Under the Lights

Jamey Boelhower

ISBN: 151152653X
ISBN-13: 978-1511526531

DEDICATION

This book is dedicated to Mr. Holt, my high school English teacher, the first person to believe in my writing. This book is also dedicated to all the athletes I've had the honor of coaching.

CONTENTS

ACKNOWLEDGMENTS

Book cover designed by Kaylee Fike
Photo provided by user bpcraddock from pixabay.com under the Creative Commons Deed CC0.

1. HISTORY

Twin Valley Public School was constructed in the 1960s to help four small towns keep some type of identity as the towns' populations started to shrink. The younger generations started to head out to the bigger cities. The movement of the youth expressing their freedom plus the call of duty of the Vietnam War took boys off the farm. The young girls started to dream of lives that consisted of bright lights and careers.

The city councils of the four towns were ahead of their time. In the summer of 1961, the towns came together to discuss the future of their communities. The biggest aspect that allowed the school to be formed was the strong farm community. Each town had its local coffee shop, bar, and gas station. However, many of the families were farmers, and land overlapped town boundary lines. The summer was not without some heated debates at the gyms of each school, but the people were not bullheaded enough to realize that small town America was changing. With a few hard feelings that healed by harvest time, Twin Valley Public School was constructed and ready by the 1964-65 school year.

The choice of the mascot was one of the most heated discussions. Each community wanted their mascot: Cardinal, Plainsmen, Bulldog, and Rattlers. But it was Nancy Kellawoski that brought the discussion to a halt. The cute little six-year-old cuddled on her dad's lap mentioned out loud during a rare moment of silence, "I like Vikings, Daddy. Twin Valley Vikings. Like your team, Daddy, that you watch on TV. That'd be a cool mascot." Silence, then laughter that released the tension in everyone. The laughter carried on for a few minutes as people considered the sound of the new name, Twin Valley Vikings. It was voted to be the mascot in a unanimous decision.

The school sat almost directly in the middle of the surrounding towns, in a pasture at the top of a rolling hill that falls into the river that runs across the state. A state highway ran by the school. Cows were sometimes spectators at football practices. The school became the pride of all the communities. It had some strong teams in every decade, but no State Champion for a team sport, even though football and both basketball teams had been runner-ups. In 1988, every team had made it to their respective state tournaments. The track team finished second, but had three state champions that year.

Everything has a cycle, and over the last ten years, the Twin Valley Vikings had not had much success. A few teams went farther then people expected, but a consistently average athletic performance had filtered into the school. Parents were always on coaches, and athletes seemed to be more concerned with game day then doing what it took in practice to be ready. Coach David Reiner was the sixth head coach in the last decade. But he was feeling good after his first season as head football coach. He grabbed his wife's hand on the table and took in the atmosphere.

The tables held an array of different colored shaped dishes. The aroma still lingered in the air. Most of the football players were making their way back to the selection of chicken, homemade casseroles, brownies, and other goodies. David was tempted to get another plate. Especially Mrs. Dansen's fried chicken. But he had gotten his hands clean and didn't want his stomach too full for when he had to speak and hand out honors for the football team.

The gym was slowly filling with noise as parents finished their plates, and little brothers and sisters found their way to playing tag around the outside of the gym, the parents hushing their child as they ran by but to no avail. Coach Reiner watched the kids play for a minute, amazed at how life was so simple for them. They knew only that they could run and play. Coach Reiner smiled as a Nerf football magically appeared. Football was just a game, but Coach Reiner had been involved with football since fourth grade either as a player or a coach. It was the perfect combination of individual strength and courage matched with team mentality and goals. When players did their best, the team had success. Every play was a moment of truth, for the player, for the coach, for the team. With each snap, success or failure was an equal option.

Dr. Stevenson made his way to the podium. James Stevenson was the superintendent of Twin Valley High School. He was engaged in most aspects of the school. He would walk the halls during passing periods. He was seen at most sporting events, even if it wasn't his turn to do crowd patrol. He attended elementary programs and even once played the piano for a Christmas concert when the choir teacher was hit with the flu. This was Coach Reiner's first job, but he knew that Dr. Stevenson went above and beyond his contract duties for the school.

Dr. Stevenson made some welcoming remarks and then introduced Mrs. Welk, the cross-country coach. Mrs. Welk did her best with the seven athletes that came out for Cross Country. Football and Volleyball attracted most of the athletes in the school. Mrs. Welk had two girls and one boy make it to state. She expressed her excitement for the future of the team. All three of the state qualifiers were sophomores, and they were only losing one senior.

Next was Ms. Ann Stellway. She was a fiery woman, standing 6 feet tall. She always kept her hair back because she had no qualms jumping in to show the girls how to do something on the court or the classroom. She had been at Twin Valley for three years. She had played collegiate volleyball at Colorado State, but had gone to high school in Grand Island and wanted to come home for her career. She expressed how proud she was of how the team had finally started to come together. They had stormed the district tournament, losing in the finals; but because they didn't have enough wild card points, they missed the state tournament. The team would be losing seven seniors, but had a strong junior class and the upcoming freshman and sophomores were a talented bunch.

Next was football.

Coach Reiner could not believe he was feeling emotion tighten his throat as he walked to the make shift podium. But he felt the weight of pride as he looked out across the gym. This was the beauty of high school football. The row of tables with families and athletes bustling with conversation, the buffet of homemade food that would rival any restaurant. The kids, ignoring their parents, played on the other side of the gym. This is why he wanted to coach high school football, to be a part of a community, to watch as players grew and developed into men. His first year as head coach was a good year, not great. They would never make a movie out of the season, yet they were building something. And he was the coach.

The gym fell silent as Coach Reiner cleared his throat, "We had a handful of goals set for this season… that we did not reach." The gym's energy fell. The football players' eyes drifted from each other to the table in front of them.

"It has been thirteen years since Twin Valley has won the

season opener, it has been seven years since we have had a .500 or better record. We did not play consistent in our games. We did not play this season to our potential." The seniors seemed to fidget in their seats, a few with growing frowns. The gym was now dead silent, the crowd not prepared for such a negative speech for the fall awards night. Coach Reiner could see the confused and somewhat angry look on some of the fathers' faces, especially Charlie Allen's face. Charlie was Troy's dad, and it had been a rough year between him and Charlie.

Coach Reiner paused, he believed in honesty. No football player, or any other person for that matter, could grow if they were not honest with themselves. He let the moment stay, to let the players think about the past and what could have been. A slight rustle could be heard from the tables. He continued his speech before he lost them.

"Yet," a smile breaking on his face despite the fact he did not want to show it yet, "we, as a team, have turned a corner. We accomplished a handful of goals, winning homecoming for the first time in eight years, having our first shut-out on defense, and ending the season four and five, after only one win in the last four years."

The energy rose just as quickly as his smile. The football players jostled with each other with the memory of the good things they had done. Parents turned to their sons with smiles. Coach Reiner let them have the moment.

"And finally," the gym quickly became hushed, but with a buzz, "we have started… started to build one heck of a good football team." The buzz was released and the gym filled with applause. This was the beauty of high school football.

2 PRESEASON

Jason hit the off button on his alarm. He had been up for the last 20 minutes anyway. He was usually up already doing chores, but his dad said he would cover the chores this week. But only this week. Jason lay there feeling a mixture of excitement and dread. It was the first day of two-a-days.

The smell of bacon and eggs got him going. Jason smiled. He loved breakfast. He knew his family was different in that they always ate breakfast together. The evenings were too busy; his dad would be out working on something on their ranch, or at grandpa's farm. The last couple of years had been tough, as grandpa's health had deteriorated. Running a cattle ranch plus 500 acres of corn took time. The whole family chipped in, his two uncles had their own farms, but it was still difficult getting everything done.

Jason stretched. He searched for a pair of shorts and his Twin Valley football shirt. Coach Reiner only allowed school shirts for practice, which Jason thought was weird last year, but now understood the pride aspect Coach was trying to instill. During the first practice last year half the team practiced in the colored pennies because they had worn shirts that advertised other schools. It took two weeks before everyone remembered to wear Twin Valley gear to practice.

"Jason, breakfast is ready. Let's not be late on the first day!" his dad hollered up the stairs.

"I'm on my way," Jason replied as he pulled on his socks.

Father and son sat across from each other. Almost a mirror image. Blond hair that was cut short, Dan's hairline a little thinner than his son's. Both of them had strong cheekbones and broad shoulders from baling hay, working fence, and just natural build. The biggest difference between father and son was their smile. Dan smiled easily, even when life was tough. Son rarely smiled; Jason approached everything with an attitude of seriousness. It didn't mean Jason didn't enjoy life; in fact Jason was excited for his senior year. Just that Jason was serious about everything he did.

"Dad, would you pass the orange juice?"

"Yeah, here you go." Dan stuck the bacon strip between his lips to grab the cantor of juice. "Ready for practice?"

"Yeah, I can't wait for the season to start though. To play. I would love to get to the playoffs this year. We should easily be 6-3. Last year one team made it to the playoffs with a losing record."

"The wildcard system has some unique aspects to it. The football system is a lot different now then it was when I played. But don't get ahead of yourself. You know all you can control is your effort. You can't count on the wildcard points." Jason looked up from his scrambled eggs as to say he had heard this before. Dan continued, "But it would be nice to see how far this team can go." Jason cracked a rare smile.

"I think you will have a great season." Jason's mom, Teresa, added. "I like what Coach Reiner is doing with the program."

The men nodded their agreement. Jason's phone went off. He checked the screen to see that Teon had texted him. "It's Teon." All three of them broken into smiles. Teon was family, now, but it wasn't always so.

Teon Witte was an option student from the city of Kearney.

Teon drove thirty miles one way to the school. When needed, he stayed with the Petersen's. Jason and Teon were the odd couple in the school. A friendship born two summers ago. Teon Witte was a sophomore when he opted into Twin Valley. It was the simple story of having the wrong friends and nothing to do after school. Teon had that instant charm, too much energy, and no father to guide him. His junior high and freshman years in Kearney found Teon lost in the system and loving the freedom that came with it.

Angel Witte had worked as a secretary in the admission's office for the community college for over ten years. During that time, she had met a number of students from Twin Valley and was always impressed with their overall attitude and preparation for life after high school. It was a battle, but Teon started the second quarter of his sophomore year as a Twin Valley Viking.

The battle continued all that year. Teon was the only black student in the high school. The elementary population was growing in its diversity as younger families started to move into the area and commute to the bigger cities. Grand Island was about 40 miles east. However, the high school's population was not diverse. The first day he felt as if he was walking naked through the school. He could almost hear the thoughts of the students, their eyes sending out waves of judgments. Teon hid his fear and fronted with a "do-not-care" attitude.

Teon was smart enough to play the system. He skipped school, but never too much. He simply asked people for their homework to check his answers. No one said no. He thought he had it made until he ran into his mom at Subway during a school day in late February. He tried to talk his way out, but Angel wouldn't be swayed.

The battle changed. Angel drove him to school and to help with her job schedule, Teon went out for track, against his wishes. Teon was long in the limbs, but confident in his movements, and Coach Stan Benford saw a high jumper. Teon had minor success right away. But that success was confronted the day he and Jason almost got into a fight on the bus ride home from a track meet.

Jason was a thrower; his years of working on the farm had developed his strength. He was relatively quick, which was why he played left tackle, to protect Mike's blindside. He did not dislike Teon, he just hated how over the top he acted, especially as Teon started to improve and place at meets. Teon had placed third at the meet and was bragging it up. It grated on Jason's simple attitude of working hard and having pride in the work.

A few seats back from Teon, in an exasperated sigh, Jason said, "Just shut up already. You got third."

The bus went silent. Jason was only a sophomore, but because of his size and work ethic, he was respected in school.

"What'd you say?" Teon asked standing up, trying to not show the sudden disappointment that he felt. He had gained some friends; people seemed to like him. This was the first time anyone had, at least to his face, challenged him.

Jason stood. They were both over six-foot, but Jason's shoulders overshadowed Teon's. Coach Benford turned around, hands on the back of his seat, but decided to let the situation play out.

Jason set his eyes on Teon, "I said shut up. You got third, but you're acting like you won the damn track meet."

Teon cocked his head to the right and stepped into the aisle. Coach Benford tightened his grip, but stayed in his seat. "Don't you worry none, I'll win the whole damn thing. And talk about it all I want." A small rustle from the kids around them.

Then it was matched with a slight rumble from the seniors in the back, a whispered, "Get him, Jason."

"If you would actually work at high jump, you would win the high jump." Jason's voice was calm, but his hands started to clench. He kept his eyes on Teon. The tension was building. Everyone was shocked, not by Teon's attitude but by Jason's. He was known to be a no nonsense kid. A hard worker, great teammate, but low key. Choosing not to talk but to let his actions speak for him.

"What? I am working, big man." Teon's pride had been struck. He kept eye contact with Jason as his mind raced about his next move. He thought he was taking things, taking life seriously, but now this kid was fronting on his performance. Plus, this kid hardly ever said anything, hardly smiled, but now was all over his case.

In a matter of fact voice Jason said, "Teon, you could be so much more than what you are right now, but you care more about everyone seeing you then actually bettering yourself." Jason felt everyone looking at him, he decided it was over He had made his point, so he sat back down and fell silent as he stared out the window.

Teon stood there a second, actually hearing what Jason said, but then replied, "Whatever, you just wait and see." However, Jason's words were running through his head.

But that was just the start, as school ended Jason's dad informed him that they were going to have an extra hand on the farm during the summer. Did he know the Teon Witte kid? Jason closed his eyes. Yes, he knew him. It seemed that Angel Witte had contacted the guidance counselor, Mrs. Turner, about an opportunity for Teon to work maintenance at the school during the summer. There were not any openings for summer maintenance, but Mrs. Turner said she had an idea and contacted Dan. They had been friends since elementary school. After hearing the situation, Mr. Petersen thought it would be a great idea to help Teon out.

The battle started as soon as Teon showed up for work thirty minutes late. But changed just as quickly when Dan took off his gloves and looked down at Teon.

"Son, I agreed to giving you a job. I can just as easily unagree to it. You get no more warnings." Dan handed him a set of gloves. "We need to get this fenced fixed. Put those on, and let's get to work." Teon stood there deciding what path to take. You could see his eyes flicker from disbelief of standing out in a field being reprimanded to jumping to the comfort of his "do-not-care" attitude and just walking away. Then he decided.

"I can fix a fence."

It would be nice to say that the summer went smoothly, but for the month of June it seemed that Jason was spending more time fixing what Teon was supposed to do than his own jobs. And even Mr. Petersen had to ask if Teon was ever silent. Teon would be sprawled out, winded, aching, and would still talk about what he had done that day. But somehow, by the first of August, Teon and Jason were not only co-workers but would soon be teammates.

Coach Reiner had talked Teon into coming out for football right before two-a-days started. Coach Reiner wanted to try to have as many of the boys in school out for football as possible his first year. He would let practice and the demands of football weed them out. However, he felt that if they would get a true taste of the game, he would have them hooked. Teon hated practices, but he loved the games. And it was during the St. Michael's game that changed Jason and Teon's relationship.

The Knights were perennial powerhouse. A Catholic school that had been to the playoffs for twelve straight years, winning the state title twice.

Teon had got to talking too much. But Jason respected his attitude toward the Knights, and grudgingly respected how Teon played the game with his heart. Others on the football team seemed to have just laid down and died during the game. Despite what Coach Reiner was trying to change his first year. Jason was getting fed up with the chatter from the Knights, too. Despite the team losing, and losing bad, Teon and Jason became strong friends during game.

It was the third quarter, the Knights were up 34 to 0, but Twin Valley was moving the ball, again. It just seemed that God liked the Knights, as every time the Vikings got rolling something negative would happen. A fumbled snap, a holding penalty, something. It was third and short on the Knights 46-yard line. Coach Reiner called Twins Left, 8-3-B 24 Fake Dive. A play action pass with Teon coming over the top as the slot receiver. God must have told the right side linebacker what the play was because he did not bite on the fake dive.

Mike's pass was just a little ahead of Teon, who had cut the route a little short to sit between the linebacker and the free safety. Teon could have let the ball fall, but instead, he made the judgment to lay out to catch the ball as his body went parallel to the ground. With the ball grasped, Teon pulled his hands to his chest as he landed. The right linebacker went head first at Teon as he curled with the ball, just missing hitting Teon in the head but smacking him in the back. Teon instantly arched, but still held on to the ball.

Jason had seen the catch and the hit. The frustration bubbled. He was tired of losing, he was pissed at most of the team for being doormats, and to see such an obvious cheap shot on a teammate sent him over the edge. He waited to see a flag or something from the ref as he sprinted to the spot, but nothing. The free safety, number 14, was getting up, yapping something to his fellow Knights when Jason reached him. The free safety had turned back toward Teon to say something as Teon was trying to get up when Jason grabbed him with both hands and lifted him a few inches off the ground. Face to face, Jason muttered, "Back off!" Then he threw the kid to the ground before he could even take a breath.

Jason was slammed in the back, but only turned around. The Knight's middle linebacker was shouting profanities. Just like that, there was a mix of players shoving and yelling. The referee's whistle sounded weak against the energy of the young men. Jason stood his ground as the shoving became frantic. Then suddenly from his right, a flash of purple and black took out the Knights' middle linebacker who had just mentioned something about Jason's mother. Teon had come up hitting.

There were a number of flags, but they all seemed to cancel each other out. The Vikings had the first down but did not score. In fact, they lost forty-four to nothing. However, that un-teachable bond had been formed for the team, and for Jason and Teon. They would become Twin Valley's version of the odd couple

Mike Olsen hit the snooze for the fourth time. He was excited to start football; he just was not a morning person. That moment between doing what you know needs to be done or succumbing to the temptation of a warm blanket loomed in his head like a wave. Grudgingly, he pushed himself from the wave and walked to the bathroom.

Mike washed his face, brushed his teeth, and cleaned up the stubble on his cheeks. He combed his thick black hair, added spritz to hold the look. He kept himself looking clean, looking good. Mike smiled easily, but his eyes always seemed to be focused elsewhere.

When they did center in on someone they felt lost in the gold and green speckles of his eyes. Mike seemed to be able to measure and judge a person or situation in a glance. That was one of the reasons he was so good at the quarterback position. The other reason was his attention to detail. From the silence in the house he knew his mom must be just finishing her shift as a nurse at the hospital and was driving home. She worked the seven p.m. to seven a.m. shift in the critical care unit in Kearney. He worried about her. He knew the job paid well. She volunteered for extra shifts so that they could make ends meet.

His mom and dad had divorced when he was ten. Mike hadn't seen his father since. He got one birthday card when he turned eleven. In it was twenty dollars and a promise his dad would come see him for a visit. He spent the money on a PlayStation game but never got the visit from his dad.

Mike grabbed a Pop-tart on the way out the door. Mike stopped and wrote a quick “Love you” on their message pad on the refrigerator.

Troy crept through the house trying to find a t-shirt to wear to practice. He knew better than to wake either of his parents, but he was getting agitated. Troy was counting down the days until he could leave this mess. He shifted through the pile of laundry, smelling shirts until he found one that he could stand wearing. Luckily, it was a Twin Valley shirt. The last thing he wanted was for Coach to make him an example of the t-shirt rule. He was sure there was going to be a freshman or two who would show up wearing some other school's logo on their clothes. Coach would have a day with them.

Troy looked in the fridge and cupboards for something to eat. It just made him angrier. He toasted some bread and scraped the last of the peanut butter onto it. He was simply ashamed of his parents and the house. He couldn't remember the last time he had friends over.

Troy took a deep breath as he stood on the doorstep. The sun was sitting on the horizon; he had about ten minutes to make it to practice. He was ready, if for nothing else to forget about things for a while.

Coach Reiner was sipping coffee. The apartment was dark except the light over the stove. He was already feeling the anticipation of the first practice. He felt good. The team had about 90 percent of the kids in the weight room over the summer. He even played a few times when the boys played touch football games on Tuesday nights during the summer. He downed the last bit of coffee, rinsed out the cup, and left it in the sink. He then walked the few feet to their bedroom to give his wife a kiss. Even if she was sleeping, she always wanted a kiss goodbye. He swore she was dead asleep the first time he snuck out of the house without kissing her goodbye. When he returned she was on his case because he had not kissed her goodbye. He had never left the house without kissing her since then.

"Ready?" she mumbled as he bent down to kiss her.

"I think so." He sat down on the edge of the bed.

"Hmm, I think this could be a good year. Are we still going out tonight for dinner?" Julie turned from her side to her back to look at David.

"Yes. Yes, we are. But not until after seven. Tonight's practice starts at 4:30. But we won't go the full two hours, and I'll need to shower."

"OK. If I'm not here when you get home, I'm at school working in my room." Julie taught fourth grade for the Twin Valley district. This was the first teaching job for both of them. They had met in college. David had asked Julie out after a debate in an educational class they were both in. They had been on opposite sides of the class debate, the role of parental input regarding discipline guidelines for the classroom.

At the end, it was just them debating, the rest of the class silent but in awe of the energy in the room. Both of them snapping off statistics and philosophy as the debate simply came down to the moral obligations of a teacher in a society that did not always provide those guidelines. Their grade level of teaching kept them separate, David pressing for more student responsibility in their own development and Julie standing strong that without the guidelines directing the students, they couldn't develop the freedom to be self-disciplined.

It was love at first site, well on David's side. Julie was not so free with her heart, yet they were married within two years of their first date.

"Alright, I got to go," David said.

"Love you," Julie said as she sat up to kiss him.

"Love you." David headed out the apartment as the first rays of the sunrise broke the darkness. He thought to himself, this is the year.

3 IN SEASON

The morning had a different feel; it was the first practice with pads. Three days of running drills, learning plays and schemes, and conditioning had come to this moment. When football was played. Coach Reiner knew that this first practice would probably reveal how this season truly went. There was something about the first practice with pads that separated the players from the participants. To see who wanted to play and who wanted to stand on the sideline would be determined this morning. He smiled.

"Oh boy, can't wait to hit some freshmen," Troy Allen hollered as he jumped out of his truck.

"Maybe later, Troy," Coach Reiner hollered back.

"Coach, come on, you know they need to know how it feels to play varsity football." Troy was grabbing his gear out of the bed of his truck. He was smiling. His smile brought you in. His dark eyes would encompass you so that you felt like you were best friends. But he could change in an instant. Troy's eyes would narrow, his smile turned to a thin line; you didn't want to be in his line of sight when Troy had that look.

"They will, they will." Coach Reiner glanced over to the small huddle of freshmen. They were wide-eyed through their facemasks. Each one staring at Troy. They knew who he was.

Everyone knew Troy. He came from a tough family situation. His mom and dad were together, but both were known to have relationships outside their marriage. Both were drinkers, just at different bars. Troy's dad, Charlie, had a mean streak when drunk. Last year there was a tense face off after the second game of the year between Charlie and Coach Reiner.

Charlie had shoved Troy to the ground when Troy had stepped into the situation. Coach had benched Troy in the third quarter because he was stepping away from the plays as a linebacker. Coach Reiner was afraid. He could hear Charlie from the stands. He knew Charlie was drunk. It took everything Coach Reiner had to stand strong as Charlie had run him down grabbing him by the collar and started yelling at him after the game. Coach Reiner was taken by surprise. The quickness and venom behind Charlie's words froze Coach Reiner to the spot.

Troy was not far behind. He knew what his dad could do. As Charlie's voice rose, and his hands continued to push or point at Coach Reiner, Troy stepped in between them. Coach Reiner had stayed silent, strong on the outside, but shaking like a leaf on the inside. He was quickly trying to figure out how to get out of the situation, when Charlie grabbed his son by both shoulders, picked him up, and dumped him to the ground. Not an easy thing to do. Troy was a few inches taller than his dad. Troy was just over six foot, but you could see where Troy got his strength when you looked at his father. Both of them had shoulders that could carry the weight of the world, arms that had that natural chiseled muscle tone. Charlie turned back to Coach Reiner. Coach Reiner was about to say something; he didn't know what actually, but he needed to do something.

"Coach was right to bench me, Dad," Troy said picking himself up off the ground.

"No. No Allen has ever been benched," Charlie turned back to eye Coach Reiner. "That doesn't happen."

Coach Reiner steadied himself, "I understand you're..."

Charlie didn't let him finish. "You don't understand anything." Charlie seemed ready to end the discussion with his fist.

"Dad," Troy's voice was strained and exhausted. "Dad, Coach was right… I wasn't playing like I should have." Charlie turned toward his son, face still filled with rage. Troy looked at his dad hard, "I didn't step up." Then Troy walked away leaving his dad and Coach Reiner standing there. Coach Keller and Coach Sanders were now a few feet away.

Charlie stood there, seeming not to have heard his son. When he turned back to Coach Reiner, he said in a low voice, "You will never bench my son again."

Charlie's fists were clenched the whole time he walked across the parking lot.

Coach Reiner tried to calm his nerves, but he was shaking so bad that his pen had shaken loose from his clipboard. He bent down to pick it up. Troy was never benched again, but not because Coach Reiner was afraid of Charlie. Troy kept himself in games by the way he played. There was now an unspoken truce between Coach Reiner and Charlie. When they crossed paths around town, they simply nodded.

Troy was a little too loud, had too many side comments in class, yet you could see through the act. Understandably, Troy seemed to be battling a ghost that was determined to bring him down.

"Let's get this day going." Coach Reiner yelled. The team took a few extra seconds to get settled into their warm up lines, as they straightened their gear to their right.

"Count'em out loud…"

"It's hot, gentlemen. The plan is to hit it hard for an hour. This morning we went through all the instructional drills: Perfect Fit, Side Line Tackle, Angle Tackling. It's time to put some pop into those pads." The upperclassmen jostled with each other in agreement. "But remember, we are a team. No cheap shots, everything is clean. Everything is done right," he paused. "On the line."

The team exploded to the two tackling boxes already set up. To start, they separated into upperclassmen and lower classmen. Coach Keller was already barking at the younger players. "Too tall.

Drop the hips. This is not a dance." Coach Reiner smiled; he knew Coach Adam Keller had a teddy bear heart, despite his imposing figure. Coach Keller had played division two football, defensive end. He was already on the coaching staff when Coach Reiner got to Twin Valley last year. He had been the defensive coordinator for the last eight years, but had been a part of the football staff for twelve years.

In the interview process, Coach Reiner had asked Coach Keller why he didn't want to become head coach. Coach Keller responded that he wanted to coach, not have to deal with all the administrative aspects of the job. After just one season, Coach Reiner understood his response, however, he was happy to have him on the staff.

The other square was ripping through easily with a few tips coming from Coach Robert Sanders. Coach Sanders was the school's head boys' basketball coach. He was a scholar of both games but truly loved basketball. Coach Sanders had started at Twin Valley last year with Coach Reiner. They basically agreed on what it took for a team to succeed. Heart, team first, and hard work. They disagreed on motivation. Coach Sanders had a side to him that would rear its head when things did not go right. He could verbally strip a player down within seconds. There were times for an athlete to face the brutal truth of their effort, but Coach Reiner thought Sanders crossed that line at times. He could not begrudge the success Coach Sanders brought to the basketball team, though. The basketball team had gone from an average team to making it to the second round of sub-districts in one year.

Coach Reiner stepped in with Coach Keller and blew his whistle.

"OK, stop. As the back runs to the cone, you have to aim just ahead of him. Break down, left, right, left. See how my left leg is now in front?" The young group stared at him. "This would be when you say, yes, coach or no, coach."

In a small half muddled response he could hear, "Yes, Coach."

"What? Be strong in all you do, even if it is just an answer." Coach Reiner set his eyes on them.

"Yes, Coach!" Better, but still unsure.

"Now, as you place that left foot in front, your arms shoot from the hip, driving your right shoulder into their ribs." Coach Reiner set his body into Conner's side with a sure pop. "Look at my head placement. No different from this morning. Ears on numbers, eyes on horizon. Then as you run through him, grab jersey. Understand?"

Another soft, "Yes, Coach."

"What?" Coach Reiner let Connor go and turned quickly.

"Yes, COACH!" the players yelled.

"You got'em, Coach Keller," said Coach Reiner.

"Let's go men, Connor back to the front." Coach Keller was getting into the zone. His arms demonstrating as the players repeated the drill, barking commands as they moved.

Coach Reiner walked over to the drinking trough. A coach always had to take a deep breath with underclassmen.

"No, your head does not go on the back numbers. Were you watching as Coach just showed you how to do it?" Coach Keller was in the middle of the square overshadowing the players. Sometimes you had to take a couple of deep breaths.

The overall energy was good through practice; the promise of the black shirts had interjected some purpose to the afternoon. The black shirt was actually a black practice jersey awarded to players who showed hard work and positive team actions. Coach Reiner brought the idea with him from his own high school experience. The jersey could also be taken away. There were a few interesting parent conversations last year when a couple of seniors got their jerseys taken away during the week after their sixth game, which was a loss. The team was two and four. It made the point and things started to click. They won the next two games to reach .500. One of the victories was a shutout. They lost the last game, but the season had turned, and all the upperclassman had their black shirts.

Coach Reiner still felt the pain of that last game. He had decided to go for it on a fourth and two during the third quarter. They were behind by 5, and at their own 43-yard line. They fumbled the center-quarterback exchange. The Cardinals' defense swept up the ball and ran untouched for the touchdown. Game over. The team just did not rebound from that moment.

4 PREGAME

"Man, what a week," Mike said as he stretched out on Jason's truck bed.

"I'm tired, but that good tired. Like a hard day on the farm. I know I got something done," Jason said.

The boys were parked at The Bend. The river made a sweeping bend about three miles east of the school. It created a beach like area when the river flowed at its normal rate. During the spring, the river would actually flood the low grassland area where the kids parked their cars and trucks. A stone-based fire pit was set about 20 feet from the grass on the bend. The pit would always lose a stone or two during the spring, but once the bend was clear of the water someone would replace the lost rocks.

The Bend had been a gathering place for Twin Valley

students for generations. The Bend sat on Mr. Henson's pasture, who was now 87 years old. His son, Gerald started the tradition of meeting at The Bend when he was a junior in 1967. Gerald and a few buddies decided to camp out in the grassland. The beach area was only about 30 feet to the water and ran 30 yards along The Bend at that time. As time has a way of doing, the river continued to push the east edge and the beach area grew from the grass to the river. It was a great place for the students to congregate. There were a few simple rules that all the kids followed: close the gate at the road, keep the area clean, and do not mess with the cows.

The summer of 1981 saw The Bend closed to students when a party got out of hand, and one of Mr. Henson's cows was found inside the post office. Without ceremony it reopened the summer of 1983, when Mr. Henson's nephew Jay started his sophomore year. Jay simply asked, with the promise that nothing would happen again, if he could campout on The Bend. Nothing major had happened since, except for the occasional party with a tear-filled break-up of a couple or an occasional stuck car.

The first handful of stars was starting to shine as a car drove into the lowland with a low bass thump.

"It's Teon," both Mike and Jason said as they jumped down to meet him.

The smoke from the grills was intoxicating. Coach Reiner felt more at ease this year with the community BBQ. Last year he was flooded by parents, fathers and mothers alike, wanting to know what his offensive philosophy was. Did he know about their son's athletic ability? What was he going to do about the weight room? Their son only needed a chance to play, and Coach would see how great their son was. Dr. Stevenson rescued him by having him sit with his family. The parents stopped bothering him while he ate.

This year a few parents still chatted up their sons, mostly the parents of underclassmen. But most people simply stopped to say hi and ask what he thought the season would hold. A few even commented on specific games or plays. Coach Reiner felt he had started to build a solid reputation. He knew he would still need to prove himself, to continue to make the team better this year.

The team was eating hamburgers like they were going out of style. Some of them, like Kyle, would have their hamburger finished before they even got back to their seat.

After dinner the PTO, the Parent-teacher organization, would spend some time talking about the upcoming events that they needed volunteers for, the plans for homecoming, and other odds and ends that were the foundation of school spirit. The Athletic Boosters had a table set up with the gear for the upcoming school year: T-shirts, hoodies, and other team spirit items.

The finale to the night was the traditional family water balloon toss contest. The football players, cross country runners, and the volleyball players were in the center. Their parents were on either side. Each parent had a water balloon that they tossed to their child. Each successful toss and catch back to the parent meant that the parent had to step back to the next distance. If a balloon busted or fell the parent stopped at that distance. But the other parent kept going until they busted their balloon. The team that had the most combined distance won a free t-shirt from the booster club.

Steph, a sophomore cross county runner, beat out Jason and his parents when Jason's dad squeezed the water balloon too hard on the last throw. Coach Reiner smiled; he thought Dan did it on purpose. Dan's eyes were his downfall; they lit up when Steph hugged her dad after he caught her toss.

The whistle made a screeching halt to the practice. The team had run through their special teams, worked through the first 10 offensive of plays, covered their base defense, and were in the middle of doing down and backs.

"Ok guys, on me." Coach Reiner was standing at the 50-yard line of the practice field. The team from all over the field came jogging while snapping their chinstraps off to remove their helmets. It was a warm Thursday afternoon and the sun was shining.

You could hear the huff and puff of the boys as they settled down. Sam brought over water bottles and passed them out.

"Today is the first step to our new season. Our first pregame practice." Coach Reiner noticed how silent the world seemed as he spoke. There were no birds, no cars, nothing. It was as if the rest of the world did not actually exist. Just this team, on this field, at this moment.

"You worked really hard this summer and during two a days. We've watched game film on everyone we will face this year. All this week we have broken down the film on who we are up against and now tomorrow night is your first test. We have nine tests this season.

I know that if we bring our best effort to every Friday night that we'll be able to walk away and let the season handle itself. You've done what it's taken to be champions. We've been in the weight room, we went to summer camps, you've done the work. But the beauty and the heartbreak of sports is that they keep score and you've got to show it this Friday night. This is our team. And no matter what, we will win or we will lose, together. This is our team. Call it out!"

The team gathered to together, their hands up in the air. When Coach called out 1-2-3 and together they all hollered, "Our Team!" and headed off into the locker room to prepare for tomorrow night's game.

The coaches helped Sam and the two junior high managers, Nate and Adam, gather up the last of the equipment from practice.

Sam asked, "Are they ready, Coach?"

Coach Keller replied, "Sam, we are as ready as we'll ever be. Are you?"

"Yes, Coach, got the bag ready for you." Sam laughed. They all walked off the field ready for Friday night.

What did he expect? Troy walked in to his house to find it dark and empty. Thursday night was usually some type of dollar night for beer or something. He knew that both of his parents were out and wouldn't be home till later. He went to the kitchen to put together some food. To his surprise the cupboards and fridge were halfway stocked with food.

Troy sat at the empty table waiting for his frozen pizza to cook. He sat quietly contemplating about what next year might actually be like. He had not chosen a college or anything. He had gotten some form inquiries from some of the local colleges but nothing specific. They had mentioned football. The forms also discussed academics, but he didn't know actually what he truly wanted to do. In the moment, he just simply wanted two things; to played football and to somehow get out of this house. He wanted something more than what he had at the moment. He just didn't actually know what it was or how to get there.

Jason walked in to the house smelling his favorite dish. "Mom, is that what I think I smell?"

"Yes, I thought for your first game of the season we would make pork chops and rice." Teresa said.

Jason's dad followed through the door. "How was practice?"

Jason was kind of surprised to see his dad. He knew that he had to help Grandpa get ready for harvest, and that there were some things that needed done on their ranch.

"It was good. I think we're ready. At least it will be a better game than last year."

"I'm excited to see what you guys are going to do this year. Smells good in here. Is it time to eat?"

"In about five minutes, boys, go wash your hands," said Miranda from the dining room.

Jason's dad held up his hands and gave his son warning look. Then broke into a smile and headed into the kitchen. Jason ran upstairs to put away his school stuff and to wash his hands. Life was feeling good for Jason.

Teon drove home. Texting his mom quickly that he was on his way. He was excited. He still disliked practices, but game time was coming up and that's when he would shine. The music and miles blurred as he started to remember everything that happened in the last couple years. He thought to himself what a difference time could make. Teon was already getting of a few letters of interest to run track for some of the local colleges. Of course, his mom was on him to keep his grades up, but this year he found school to be easier, maybe because he actually took it a little more seriously. As his future started to take form in his mind he found getting things done was a little easier than before.

Teon didn't know exactly what had changed. Maybe he was just growing up, but things just seemed to matter a little bit more. He understood that he was more in control of his success and failure then he was earlier in his life. He had to admit that he was jealous of Jason and his dad's relationship. His mom told him that his dad left when Teon was seven months old. Teon had no memory of him, but he couldn't hide the fact that he wondered about where his dad might be. Funny how Teon didn't think much about his dad when things were rough, but now that Teon was doing well he thought about him. Teon shook off the thoughts. He was feeling good about life. He turned up his favorite song and headed home. He knew his mom would be there before him. He started to hope she had made something awesome for dinner.

David was chopping up the potatoes when his wife glanced over his shoulder. "Hon, are you sure this'll work?" she asked.

David turned the stove top up just a touch making sure the oil was heated. "It should work fine. I know we don't have a deep fryer but I think we can still make French fries."

Julie was not so sure. She didn't think that homemade French fries cut straight from a potato were going to work out like her husband thought. David made sure everything looked good and dumped the fries into the pan. The oil started to crackle with the potatoes right away. After a few seconds, he saw that the potatoes were starting to stick to each other. He got a fork and tried to separate the fries from each other but the oil was popping and stinging his hand. Julie sat back chuckling. David danced in front of the stove trying to avoid the popping oil. The blob of potatoes did not look like French fries at all.

David dropped the fork when his hand got hit with splat of oil. The potatoes seem to imitate the blob when it made the fork disappear. He scrambled to rinse off his hand and turned to look at his wife. He raised his eyebrows at her as if to say, *I don't want to hear I told you so*. He was looking for another utensil to better separate the fries or what was left of them. The edges of the potato mound had become dark. Smoke started to rise out of the pan.

Before David could get a new utensil, the black smoke triggered the fire alarm that sat over the doorway to the dining room: beep, beep, beep.

David grabbed a chair to stand on as he tried to turn off the smoke alarm, but it wasn't turning off. He turned the smoke alarm around to unplug the battery and the beeping went silent. He jumped off the chair, then went back to the stove and turned on the overhead fan. He looked down at the homemade fries and admitted defeat by moving the frying pan off the burner. Julie had stood there the whole time watching. Not saying a word, just letting him do his thing. She had learned that sometimes David just needed to go through with his radical ideas. And hopefully learn from them.

"Should we go to Sandy's Diner?" Julie asked while leaning on the kitchen counter with her arms crossed.

"Yeah, let me clean up here." Coach Reiner said trying actually not to laugh.

"You're getting really good at disengaging the smoke alarm,"

Julie said as she headed to get her shoes on.

Mike wasn't expecting to see his mom when he got home. But there she was making a simple dinner of grilled cheese and chicken noodle soup. Mike loved her grilled cheese sandwiches; he could never get his to taste like his mom's.

"What are you doing home?" Mike asked as he sat down at the table.

"Dee owed me a shift."

"You couldn't have taken tomorrow off?" Mike asked. His mom had not seen many games. It bothered him a little as other players parents would greet them after a game, Mike would simply walk to the locker room, knowing no one had been there to see him play.

Rachael brought over the food. "I promise I'll make a game. You know how hard it is to get my weekend shifts changed. Plus, I thought it would be nice to just be home with you."

It was nice, Mike thought biting into his sandwich. The bread was just crisp enough to let the warmth of the gooey cheese be a surprise to the taste buds. .

"I rented a movie. Even got strawberry Twizzler bites." Rachael looked at her son. What a handsome young man he was becoming. A shadow of sadness moved over her heart. This was no way for a boy to be growing up. She remembered how exhausted she was after giving birth to him, eighteen hours. But that exhaustion disappeared as soon as the nurses laid Mike in her arms. He seemed to snuggle into her chest. Gary, her husband and Mike's father, stood there beaming.

They had started out the perfect family. Rachael could not pin point when it turned. It seemed one day everything was just ruined. She and Gary were fighting all the time. Her husband seemed to work more hours, or would find something to do on the weekend. They both agreed one night that things had changed. That life wasn't working for either of them. They divorced less than a year later. She sadly thought to herself, just another classic failed marriage story.

"What movie?" Mike asked, bring her back to the present.

"Some inspirational sports movie." she replied. "You know, to get psyched for tomorrow's game."

"Sounds good," Mike said as he grabbed another grilled cheese.

5 GAME ONE

The team was quiet. Sam was handing out water bottles. The first game was always a mix of unexpected great plays and handling simple mistakes. The game was tied at 14. The Haymakers scored on two long pass plays. Plays that Coach Reiner had tried to prepare the team for. They had prepped the coverage for the Haymakers' favorite formation. It was the formation they used to score both touchdowns, but the corners had still underplayed the receivers. Coach Reiner knew they would try to hit them fast, and he was right.

The Vikings fought back though. Taking up most of the second quarter on two scoring drives that brought the game to a tie. There were some tired penalties, false starts, things like that. Over all, Coach Reiner felt good about the team's effort. Especially when they could have folded after the first quarter. He kept himself from thinking about winning the game and instead just kept the team focused on doing their best.

"How we doing?" Coach Reiner asked the team.

"Good."

"This is fun!"

"Think we can pull this off?" Coach Reiner asked.

The team didn't know how to respond. The question brought the reality of the game to them. They were tied at halftime, playing well, and victory was a real possibility. Teon spoke up, "Yea, Coach, we can pull this off."

Coach Reiner followed Teon's comment, "We need to stay focused on what we can do, which is keep our assignments on defense." Coach Reiner paused to let the team know that the blown coverage had cost them. "And do the fundamentals on offense. They get the ball to start the second half; we need stop them on their first drive. Then use our first offensive possession to score. We do that, I think we take the game."

The players turned to reaffirm his words. The energy was starting to build.

"OK, I'm going to turn it over to Coaches Keller and Sanders to cover some things, then, Troy, take them through warm ups."

"Got it, Coach." Troy said. Troy was running well. Hitting the holes quick. Coach Reiner wished he would keep his feet active a little more, make a cut, try to make the turn a few times. But Troy was hitting people, and a few of those hits broke him free for good gains.

Coach Reiner headed to the sidelines. He was trying to keep his expectations in check. Twenty-four minutes to a 1 and 0 start to the season. To winning the season opener for the first times in 13 years. He grabbed a water bottle and was greeted by a small cheer from the cheerleaders. He smiled and unscrewed the top of the bottle to get a drink.

"Think we got this, Sam?" Sam was arranging something in the med kits.

"Yes, I do, Coach."

"I think so, too."

The team was done with their halftime warm up routine. Coach Sanders was talking to Justin and Wilson, the bullets on the kickoff team. Then he gathered the kickoff team around him.

The referee blew the whistle. The team moved in a wave as the ball flew end over end. In a collision of white and crimson the teams met at the 35-yard line. The Haymakers' number 21 darted toward the Vikings' sideline, a good wall of blockers setting up in front of him. Wilson was moving toward him, no one even seeming to see him. Jason broke free of his blocker and was coming in from midfield. As Justin was breaking down in front of the returner to tackle him, a flash of crimson passed behind number 21. Wilson saw the pitch but had taken a hard inside line to tackle number 21. Wilson couldn't turn in time to even slow down number 88 as he headed for the Haymakers' sideline, turning up field with three blockers in front of him.

Coach Reiner thought it was a gutsy call, as the Haymakers' kick-returner crossed the goal line, untouched. His small wall of blockers handled Kale, the Vikings' kicker. A wave of frustration startled Coach Reiner as he started to ask himself why it was so hard to get this win, to get this season started on the right foot. He looked down at his clipboard, then to the clock. *OK, game on.*

Coach Reiner turned to Coach Sanders, "Regular kick return."

Coach Sanders looked at him for a second, and then nodded. They weren't going to try anything fancy to get the score back.

The Vikings put a solid drive together, but had to settle for a 28-yard field goal. The rest of the quarter was a stalemate, the teams exchanging punts. The third quarter ended as the Vikings had a good punt return to their own 38.

The team surrounded Coach Reiner. “Having fun?”

“Yes, Coach, but let's get some points,” Troy responded.

“I agree. Let's start with these three plays, no huddle. Everyone get to the line for the next play.”

The team moved in closer to Coach as he scripted the first three plays. A simple lead dive, a sweep, and pass set that was designed with a tight end out route. The strategy worked. Troy gained 6 yards on the dive. Then turned the corner on the sweep and was pushed out of bounds after gaining another 12 yards. The team got straight to the line, leaving the Haymakers scrambling to catch their breath as they set up their defense. Cam turned his route into a 20-yard gain.

The Viking fans were getting louder. The cheerleaders stopped cheering to watch the game. But Coach Reiner didn't hear any of it; all he could hear was the next play in his head. He was getting into his own type of zone, quickly assessing the probability of what defense the Haymakers would run and how to counter it with the best offensive play.

"Indy 36 counter."

Troy stepped left, then cut to his right just as the fullback, Brock, a junior, was heading into the three hole, Troy dashed through the six hole. He was shoved out of bounds at the Haymakers' twenty-four yard line. Coach Reiner barked out the next play. A fullback dive. The Haymakers stopped Brock after a three-yard gain. Coach Reiner decided to go for the touchdown with a flood set, three receivers to the left. The two outside receivers ran post and flag routes respectively. Mike watched for the safety's decision on the crossing of the routes. The inside receiver, Randy, would curl just under the crossing of Nick and Teon.

Nick, the outside receiver, stepped into his cut to the inside first, then Teon stepped toward the sidelines a second later. The safety backpedaled stepping with Nick, the corner sat on the curl route. Mike recognized the cover two, and saw the safety's mistake of fading to the inside. Mike planted his left foot and sent the ball to the back corner pylon.

Teon turned his head over his left shoulder; he could almost feel the corner of the end zone approaching. He glanced down, six steps at the most. He looked back and found the ball on his on his next step. The ball was coming down, but still too far in front of him. Step three. Teon decided to shorten his fourth and fifth steps and stretch out, trying to keep the feel of the turf on his feet. Reach. He watched the ball fall into his hands, then curled it into his chest as he turned a little to land on his side. The air shot out of his lungs when his body hit and slid on the ground. Teon kept the ball cradled in his arms even though he wanted to grab his sides. He turned his head to see the referee swinging his arms right to left signaling out of bounds. Teon sunk into the grass. Mike turned away, fist clenched. Just a little too much.

No gain on third down. "Field goal!" Coach Reiner barked out.

The snap was low, and the Haymakers blocked the attempt. Coach Reiner checked the clock, seven minutes, 32 seconds left. Plenty of time he thought to himself, trying to reassure himself. How could a single win be so hard to accomplish?

The Viking's defense forced a punt after seven plays, but the Haymakers ran the clock down to four minutes. Coach Reiner talked with Mike as the Haymakers punted.

“Mike, we can't just air it out.” Coach Reiner and Mike saw that the defense was already setting up a deep cover three. “We have time to run the ball, but when we do, pass it,” Coach Reiner made sure Mike was looking him in the eye, “Just throw. Don’t overthink. We don't have time for that.”

“Got it, Coach.” Mike said. His stomach felt small. His mind was filling with doubt that Mike tried to squash by concentrating on executing the next play.

The Vikings started on their own 28-yard line. Troy gained four yards on a sweep. Cam gained a first down on a dart, catching the ball on a quick throw and running for 12 yards. The Vikings crossed midfield on a second down with an inside fullback trap. The clock read three minutes 12 seconds.

First down; 5-yard pass. Second down, stuffed at the line. Third down a gain of one. The Haymakers called a timeout.

“That was a break,” Coach Reiner mentioned to Coach Keller. The team was snagging water from Sam. “OK, we are going for it. No fake punt, Indy 35 lead dive. Teon don't worry about tracking down your corner, on the snap of the ball, come inside and find the outside backer." Coach Reiner quickly drew up the play and displayed how he saw the blocking assignments. Coach Reiner tapped Teon's numbers, "Make sure your head is on his front numbers. Line, we need that hole open." Using the marker board to emphasize the linemen's job. The whole team nodded their heads. "This is why we play the game, gentlemen, for moments like this."

The team broke huddle from Coach and lined up on the ball. They knew the play. Mike set his feet. For a moment everything was crisp in Mike's view. The jerseys seemed 3D, the field a pop-up page in a book. His mouth guard felt like a big gummy bear. He could hear the crowds as a small murmur on the edges. Mike was calm in the moment.

Todd, the left tackle, called out, "Ox!" This was lineman call to take on the defenders on their outside shoulder if they are set up for a better angle. The defensive end lined head up on Cam. Jason thought to himself, *good call.* If Cam attacked the defender's outside shoulder to turn him, and Teon could reach the linebacker, then Troy just needed to follow Dean's numbers to the outside. Jason knew his assignment was to help Todd first, but his gut told him Todd could handle the tackle. Jason would go for the middle linebacker on the snap. Jason set his hand on the ground.

"Blue 87, Blue 87." Mike called, "Set. Hut!"

The ball felt weightless in Mike's hand. He stepped back with his left foot then turned to his left bringing his right foot around. Troy scraped Mike's right side as Mike popped the ball into Troy's gut and continued his steps to roll right. Mike resisted the urge to watch the play as he continued with his roll out fake.

Teon had set up a few feet in from his normal position. On the snap of the ball he headed straight for number 52. The linemen engaged the defenders, sticking the defenders' right arms, turning their center of gravity to create a walled path to the five hole. Troy stayed under control. *Follow Dean* he thought. Troy even placed his hand out to keep Dean close.

Teon flashed across Dean's facemask, hitting the linebacker square in the numbers as number 52 was setting up to take on Dean's block. Dean turned his eyes to the left finding the corner, deciding not to look inside, trusting that the mess of humanity would be enough of an obstacle for the middle linebacker.

Jason's instincts were right. Todd was able to pin the tackle's right arm. Number 64 moved up field, which was fine, Todd directed him that direction. Number 64 ended up behind the play and became a non-factor. The middle linebacker, number 55, read his keys well and was moving to his right just as Jason was moving to the second level. Jason two-arm punched him in the numbers. Number 55 countered with a swim move; his left arm chopping down on Jason's arms while jabbing Jason's shoulder with his right arm. The linebacker pushed hard to break free from Jason. Jason resisted the chop by moving in closer to the linebacker. He drove his feet to keep contact as 55 turned to his right to attack Troy coming through the hole.

Dean aimed for the corner's left shoulder. If the corner was going to make the play he would have to go under Dean. Hopefully, Troy would read Dean's numbers and break to the right and up field. Troy was in sync with Dean. Troy took a step to his left trying to bait the corner, then he cut back right and headed up field as Dean hit the corner on his left side. In the next two steps Troy bounced back toward the sideline, running untouched to the end zone.

The Viking's sideline and crowd went crazy. Unbelievable.

Coach Reiner was calling for the field goal unit when the whistle cut through the noise.

"Holding. Offense, number 67."

Coach Reiner stood there stunned. The sideline went silent, then erupted in a cascade of reactions. He couldn't see a flag. But then the side judge on the Haymakers' sideline picked up his yellow flag. Coach Reiner couldn't even think. Sixty-seven was Jason's number, there was no way he would have held on his block.

"10 yard penalty, repeat fourth down."

Coach Reiner just stood there. The whole thing wasn't making sense in his mind. He couldn't make himself believe that they were the recipients of a home field call, but he knew Jason wouldn't have held on the play. The team was standing, looking toward him. Jason had his hands out. Troy walked back, still holding onto the ball moving his head as if to ask what happened. Mike was suddenly in front of Coach Reiner.

"What's the play, Coach?"

Coach Reiner didn't have time to do anything about the call. "Viking Right A" One of their preset plays. Five receivers, with one deep route, two middle routes, and two short routes. "Watch for

Randy on the inside slant, try to lead him to the first down." Mike nodded as he headed to the huddle, his mindset still clear.

The team was huddled chatting about the last play.

"I did not hold him... I had contact on his numbers." Jason was telling everyone.

"What the... Stupid call," said someone.

"Hey! Shut up." Mike whispered hard. He was still locked in. "The play is over. We need to focus, and do it right, damn, now." That brought the team back, mostly. Mike called the play and the team set up on the ball.

"Red 27, Red 27. Set... Hut!"

The snap was a little low but manageable. The linemen set a solid pocket for Mike. The tackle tried to spin off Todd, but Jason was there and took his frustration out on him with a pancake block.

Teon was coming to the center of the field, a few yards short of the first down. Mike waited on him for a one count in his head. Randy appeared behind and to the right of the middle linebacker. Mike let the ball sail.

The middle linebacker made an incredible play by leaping to his left as the ball approached him. Football is a game of inches, sometimes half inches. The backer just nicked the ball making it turn into a duck and sending it behind Randy. Haymakers' ball, one minute 26 seconds left.

"Send'em, Coach," Coach Reiner hollered at Coach Keller. Meaning for him to blitz. The Vikings had all three time outs.

No gain on first down. Coach Reiner called the first time-out. The team gathered around him. They hadn't had time to get things figured out.

Jason was still dwelling on the hold. "Coach, I didn't hold him."

"Hey, the play is over. We need to focus, RIGHT NOW!" Coach Reiner raised his voice. "We need the ball back. I have to use all our time outs on defense or they will simply run the clock out. We won't have much time when we get the ball back or any time outs. To give us any chance, they cannot gain a first down. Do you understand?"

"Yes, Coach!" the team replied.

"Ok, men. Slant strong middle fox monster cover three. From here on out." Coach Keller barked. Coach Reiner nodded his head in agreement. Coach Reiner couldn't help but feel that deep sense of connection to the moment. The energy and expectation of the game's outcome drew them all in. They understood the moment and what needed to be done. Both coaches saw the focus in the boys' eyes. The defense allowed the middle linebacker to choose a hole to stunt through, while the strong safety covered the outside gap of the offenses' strong side.

Dean hit the A gap in sync with the snap of the ball, sacking the quarterback before he could even hand off the ball.

Time out, Vikings.

The team got water while the coaches encouraged them, two more downs and one timeout left. The Haymakers gambled with a pass play, knowing that a first down would win the game for them. Troy read the back swinging out and dropped into coverage. Jason broke free from the guard. He lunged at the quarterback's legs snagging them before the quarterback could step away from the pressure. Another sack. Coach Reiner called the last time out. One minute left. Enough time.

"I'm going to bet that they will kick the ball out of bounds. We don't have time to run, so we will go Viking formation. Let's run set B for the first play. After that, Mike, call the routes at the line."

The Haymakers punted the ball out of bounds, but it was a bad punt. The Vikings would start their last drive on their own thirty-eight yard line.

The team huddled on the field.

"OK, guys. We knew we would have to earn this win, let's go get it. Ready? Break." Mike said. He wiped his brow, no time for sweat to get into his eyes. "Green 12, Green 12." Mike scanned the defense, running the routes of his receivers quickly through his head. Seeing the play before it happened. "Set. Hut!"

The snap was low, but Mike grabbed it at his knees without much trouble. Cam was open, but he had the six-yard curl. Troy was streaking down the center, gaining the safeties' attention. Teon broke toward the sideline. Mike released the ball perfectly. Teon caught the ball and took two steps to get out of bounds at the yard marker. It gives the Vikings the first down. Fifty-one seconds left.

The team huddled up with the clock stopped.

"Viking Right, 2-5-6-8-0," Mike says, visualizing the routes in his head. They had a passing tree system for moments like this, allowing the passing plays to be customized for these situations. The routes simply went left to right through the formation.

"Set! Hut!" Mike got pressure from the right. He spun out of it, setting his feet to hit Cam running the 6 route. Gain of eight yards, but the clock was running. 48, 47, 46...

"On the ball! On the ball!" Mike was trying to get the team lined up, the receivers looked at him for the call. "Green A, Green A. Set, HUT!"

Mike had time, but no receiver seemed open. Suddenly the weight of the situation hit him. Everything looked fuzzy, panic crept into his mind. 43, 42, 41... Run. Mike took off to his right. Randy turned to block the corner, pushing him back to the middle of the field. Mike gained nine yards then stepped out of bounds. Clock read 31 seconds. They had crossed midfield.

"Stay with it," Coach Reiner told Mike as he headed out to the team huddle. Mike smiled back at him, understanding that Coach Reiner trusted him to make the right call.

Mike caught his breath. "OK, Troy, are you feeling fast?"

"Yeah, what do you have in mind?"

"Z route. Randy, you run an 8. Troy, you come underneath him. Teon, can you take the safeties with you down the center?" Teon nodded yes. "We can't get the TD with this, but we can get a good chunk of yards. Get out of bounds." Mike pointed at Troy.

"Right."

Calm had returned to Mike's mind. Making the decisions on the routes got him focused. "Green 19, Green 19. Set. HUT!"

Troy and Randy ran in sync. Both stepped inside at the same time, but after three steps Troy stepped back to the sideline. The defense was paying attention to Teon as he ran straight up the field. All the defensive backs were backpedaling to defend the deep ball. Troy nailed the timing of the route by coming just underneath Randy. The outside corner didn't move with Randy; he continued to backpedal when the two receivers broke on their routes. It was good zone defense. Mike decided to throw the ball anyway, toward the sideline.

Troy didn't pay attention to the corner. After he saw that his route was under Randy's, he looked back for the ball. The ball seemed underthrown a little, so Troy changed his route back to the line of scrimmage. He had forgotten about the defense. His concentration was on catching the ball then getting out of bounds, so when he was hit as he caught the ball and taken to the ground, he cursed in his head. The clock would stop while the chains moved, but they had to get to the line. The ball was placed at the twenty-two. The ref moved his arm in a circle to start the clock.... 19, 18, 17.

Mike was hollering out instructions. Troy tried to catch his breath and listen at the same time. Did he say the C package? The team got to the line. 12, 11, 10, 9 seconds. "Set. Hut!" Mike slammed the ball down, stopping the clock with 8 seconds left. In truth, one shot for the game.

Mike looked toward the sideline. Coach Reiner signaled Teon's number with his hands. Mike nodded.

"Catch your breath, guys." Mike slowed down his speech, feeling calm. "One shot, guys. Viking Left 2-4-6-1-9." Mike looked at Teon when he assigned him the 9 route. The team knew this was it. Teon would get the ball. By setting the strength to the left, Mike was hoping to give Teon a one-on-one match up. "Let's do this."

Teon headed down the sideline. Cam sat open in the middle on the twelve-yard line. Randy broke inside on the five, but the corner was sitting on top of the route. Mike saw the outside linebacker break free to his right. He set his feet. He knew the hit was going to hurt but let the ball fly. He didn't see the end of the play.

Teon ran, but could tell the ball was too far ahead of him. He dug in, hoping that somehow he could outrun the loss. The ball dropped deep over the back of the end zone. The Haymakers' sideline exploded. Teon kept running, tears blurring his vision.

Coach Reiner stayed at the office for little while longer. He knew his wife would probably be asleep. She knew that he hated losing. He walked around the locker room picking up small shreds of tape and other garbage, Gatorade and Power Bar wrappers.

The fourth-down holding call haunted Coach Reiner. He had the camera in his bag, but he just couldn't quite watch it yet, afraid that he wouldn't be able to find anything that called for the flag. He couldn't believe that they would get a call like that. He generally believed referees tried to do the right thing. His emotions were getting the better of him, and he took the tape out of his bag. In the office was one of those VCR/TV combination players the coaches used it for reviewing tape quickly.

He plugged in the RCA cords from the camera to the TV and fast-forwarded it to the play. On the small screen he couldn't quite tell at regular speed if the call was legit. He could see Jason making contact with number 55. Then 55 made his move toward the play.

Jason kept contact with the backer as he turned. Yes, his hands moved to the side of the linebacker, but the referee's job was to see contact established. Troy was gone by the time the linebacker was turned and pursuing the play. Coach could see that at the end of the play it could look like a hold. But Jason had no jersey in his hands; he had continued contact with the linebacker as he made his move. Coach Reiner knew that a single play wasn't the cause of the loss. The two touchdowns scored on them early played a role, but to pull off that fourth down play could have set the tone for the whole season.

Some of the most stressful aspects for coaches were the close calls. The ones that were determined by inches. A block held for one more second to spring a back. A stiff arm a second sooner to break a tackle. Or having the football outstretched towards a goal line. A coach could go crazy thinking about all the possible what-ifs in the course of a football game. Coach Reiner rubbed his forehead as the reality of losing the season opener hit him. The Vikings started the season on a losing streak, again.

Jason's dad was waiting at the school for him. The family had decided that they were heading to their grandma's house the next day.

So his dad had come to pick him up.

"Tough loss," said Dan.

"Yeah, a tough call. I didn't hold him."

"Maybe you did, maybe you didn't. The call was made. Did you feel like you did your best?"

"Yeah, I think we all played pretty well, but we wanted that win." Jason wasn't satisfied with playing well. The expectations for the team were higher than that now. His own expectations were higher than that.

"You know the only thing you can take control of is how you play. And how hard you work," Dan said.

"Yeah, Coach said something like that, too." Jason said while staring out as the truck headed out to the fields. He knew his dad was right, but the loss hurt. This was it, his last season playing high school football.

"Smart man," Dan said. He turned toward his son. They both smiled and then said, "At home Mom is getting stuff ready for the visit." After a few moments of silence Dan said, "That was one of the best games I've seen in a while."

Mike let himself into the house. He knew that his mom was at work. Sometimes he felt like a small boy walking into the house when it was completely dark. He turned on the lamp next to the door before he took off his shoes.

Mike felt horrible. He knew that that the loss wasn't all on his shoulders, but as the quarterback he knew that it was his job to lead the team.

His mind was filled with the holding call on the fourth-down play. It would be easy to blame the loss on that play, but Mike knew that he had a chance in the final minutes. He had set his feet knowing he was going to be hit. He let the ball go making sure that it wasn't underthrown. However, that is what made the ball carry beyond the end zone.

Fresh frustration started to bubble inside Mike. They were so close. At the end of the day they were starting another season with a loss. He started to wonder if anything would change. It seemed as if nothing he did made any difference.

His mom worked hard. She did her best on the job. He knew she was well respected. But things never changed in their day-to-day life. She still had to work hard to make everyday life work.

He always hoped that his father would show up at a game. That somehow his dad would hear about how well his son was playing and would come see Mike play. Just like the movies. As Mike sat on the couch, the silence of the house reminded him that this was not a movie.

Mike wanted to do something, but his body was achy, and he was feeling tired. He put his head back on the couch letting his thoughts wander. He replayed the game in his mind, but this time the flag wasn't thrown. As the team celebrated he fell into a deep sleep.

When Troy got out of the locker room with his gear, he jumped into his truck determined to find a party. After a few minutes of driving around, his body and mind felt fatigued, so he turned his truck around in the middle the street and headed for home.

Like with many of the other players and coaches, the fourth-down play was in his head. He felt that the refs totally made a home-field call. He knew Jason did his best on the play. He replayed every step of the run.

He couldn't help but feel anger rising in him. The holding call was bogus. He knew that it was one of the best plays in his football career.

When Troy got home he was feeling too tired to actually think about the game anymore. He grabbed a big glass of milk from the refrigerator and sat down in the living room. He gulped the milk down in one drink. Troy let the heaviness of his eyes take over and was soon curled up asleep on the couch.

It was 2:30 in the morning when his dad walked in. He was in a sour mood. "What a bogus call," his dad said as he plopped down on the loveseat.

His dad than rattled off some more explicit ideas about the referees and the Haymakers' team and fans. That's what woke up Troy. He could smell the heavy scent of whiskey, beer, and smoke from his dad. Troy tried to remain silent.

"I knew that it was going to be a tough game on their field," Charlie rambled on to himself. His voice slurred. Troy didn't know if his dad actually recognized that he was sleeping on the couch.

But then his dad said, "And why the hell didn't you get out of bounds on that pass play?"

Troy didn't say anything. He waited to see where this question might go. He knew that a moment like this could send his dad off the handle.

“Why didn't you get out of bounds?”

“I adjusted to make the play on the ball.” Troy was feeling pretty groggy. Being woken up like this also made him agitated.

“You should have known that you needed to stop the clock.” Charlie’s voice was starting to rise. “That coach of yours has no time management. I can't believe they hired some rookie right out of college.”

Troy kept his mouth shut. Troy had come to understand that his dad hated everything in this world. In junior high he believed everything his dad said. He had found himself hating almost everything in the world, too. But during his sophomore year his dad just started to sound idiotic.

“Is it now 14 years since we won the season opener?” Charlie asked, knowing the answer.

Troy again didn't say anything because it looked as if he was talking again to himself. Troy decided just to go to bed. He stood up and walked past his dad when Charlie grabbed his arm.

“You should've got out of bounds. That was a horrible decision.” Troy’s dad held onto his arm as he stood up. Charlie’s legs were a little wobbly, but his grip was steel.

Troy felt a surge of panic. His dad could be verbally mean, but he had never been physical before. Charlie's grip was actually starting to hurt. Troy tried to shake free.

"Dad, I want to go to bed." Troy shook his arm. His dad stared at him. But he let go of Troy's arm.

"It was a stupid play. Your coach is a joke." Charlie sat back down in the chair. As Troy headed to his bedroom, he thought he could hear his dad sleeping. A low rumbling snore was coming from the living room.

While Troy got undressed he started to shake. He was coming down off the adrenaline of the moment with his father. Somehow the tiredness of life seemed to hit his back. He sat on the bed wondering if anything would ever change.

6 GAME TWO

The bus was quiet. The storm had ended, but the clouds stayed to make the road home as dark as the mood on the bus as everyone pondered starting the year 0 and 2. Even worse, the game had been a disaster.

Coach Reiner stared out the window. North Star Catholic was a solid team, but not out of their league. He knew it would take a great effort to capture the win, but after the effort in the first game he thought they were ready. He was wrong.

Coach Sanders moved to his edge of the seat to talk with Coach Reiner. "It was the craziness at the beginning, Coach. They lost focus, and we never got it back."

That was an understatement. The game went into the mercy rule a few minutes into the third quarter. If a team was up by 45 points there would be a running clock for the rest of the game. The Vikings got 45 ruled once last season by St. Michael's, the best team in the area.

We shouldn't have lost focus. That was my fault, Coach Reiner thought to himself as he stared out the window. Every once and a while you could see light shining in a window, or from a light pole outside a barn. Coach Reiner was battling a voice in his head. It simply repeated that he had failed. It sounded a lot like Troy's dad Charlie's voice, which was audible during the second half, until Dr. Stevenson and Mr. Harrison had a conversation with him. Luckily, Charlie left after that. Coach Reiner was afraid there would be another confrontation. After the way Charlie had made a scene, Coach Reiner feared it would have been a physical confrontation.

"We'll regroup, Coach." Coach Sanders touched his shoulder. Coach Reiner nodded his head and then turned back to the darkness outside the bus window. The whole situation filled his thoughts.

North Star was having an early homecoming game. The student body was milling around the open space in front of the Viking's locker room. The visitor's locker room was on the far side of the gym. The team had to walk along the outside gym wall to the gate that opened into the football stadium. The student body always congregated there during warm ups. Some wouldn't even move out of the way as the team headed to the field. Coach Reiner made sure a coach went with any of the players to and from the locker room. He didn't need any confrontations between players and students.

There was a chance of storms rolling through the area, but it was supposed to be a light rain and pass quickly. With ten minutes left before kick-off, a storm came through with lightning, the kind that flashed and rumbled continually. The stadium was emptied. The coaches were informed that the referees would wait 20 minutes after the last lightening strike before they would continue warm ups. The teams were sent to the locker rooms.

That's where Coach Reiner knew he had lost his team. He had never had to handle a team through a delay like that. Instead of meeting in groups to discuss game plans, or walking through plays, he let them relax. Coach Reiner thought that if the boys relaxed they would conserve energy for the game and would be able to get psyched for the game once the storm passed. Before he knew it, he had to round them up from the hallway or from the open area by the gym. The main problem was the girls hanging around the locker room. The boys were being boys, acting cool and macho to gain the girls' attention. The team totally lost their focus.

They had no chance once the game started.

Coach Reiner rubbed the bridge of his nose, then his left temple. He knew the blame was his. He learned a lesson. He promised himself that he wouldn't let distractions get the best of him or his team again.

A small rumble of laughter escaped from the back.

"Right now is not a time for laughter, gentlemen." Coach Keller spoke for Coach Reiner. Coach Keller understood, too. Becoming great was an everyday thing.

The bus fell silent.

7 GAME THREE

Coach Reiner was irritated. He blew his whistle. "Let's do it again."

He was totally disappointed in the attitude of the team. They were lackluster and unfocused. The offense couldn't do more than gain a couple yards on any play. The receivers dropped the ball. What was worse was the attitude they had when they came back to the huddle. The players were kidding around, acting as if it was cool to make a mistake.

"Let's do it again!" Coach Reiner just about threw his clipboard to the ground but tried to hold onto his cool.

The offense ran a simple counter; the line did a good job opening a hole for Troy to run through but instead of darting that way he just ran into the defense. Coach Reiner blew his whistle loudly, “Water break!”

Coach Reiner turned to face the sideline, not moving a muscle. Coach Keller and Coach Sanders encouraged the team to get their drinks a little bit faster. They knew Coach Reiner was upset.

The team got a drink. They halfheartedly jogged back and gathered around Coach Reiner. They were jostling with each other, and Troy made some remark about a freshman's mom.

“Take a seat.” Coach Reiner continued to gather his thoughts. He wanted to just erupt on them. To call them out, but he kept that temptation at bay.

The team settled around him in a horseshoe formation, continuing to jostle each other, goofing around a little bit waiting for Coach Reiner to speak.

“Is this who we are?”

The team settled down at the question, but a few players still goofed off. Troy and Kyle were not paying attention at all.

“I'll ask the question again for those individuals who have decided that goofing off is more important … and maybe that's the answer. Is this who we are?”

Troy and Kyle stopped whispering to turn their attention to

Coach.

"Is this who we are?" Coach Reiner stood there, his hands on his hip, waiting for an answer. He let time tick away.

The team became restless. Coach Reiner just stood there waiting for an answer. Coach Keller and Coach Sanders waited on the wings. It was less than a minute since Coach Reiner asked the question, but it felt like ten minutes.

"What do you mean, Coach?" Teon asked.

"As a football team, as a member of this team, is this who we are?" Coach Reiner was going to let the question sit for a little bit longer. His anger was being held at bay, but the silence of the team was pushing his disappointment in them. Another twenty seconds went by, and Coach Reiner couldn't wait any longer.

"We have the same record as last year, and yet, you guys are practicing as if you don't care."

The team shifted their weight. Facing the truth always made people uncomfortable, but without it there's no way to improve. Each of the players glanced at each other then back to Coach Reiner.

"There are over 100 football teams in the state practicing right now. There are teams that traditionally have winning records.

There are teams that traditionally have losing records. They're all teenage boys; they all have goals and aspirations. So what's the difference between a losing tradition and a winning tradition?"

Coach Reiner let the last question sit for a second. He was going to ask for an answer, but talking was ebbing his anger so he continued, "The simple difference is wanting to be a champion."

"Everybody is practicing right now. Everybody is doing reps. Every team is game planning for the next opponent. The teams with winning traditions are wanting to win. They are putting their heart and pride on the line to be champions. That is the difference. They simply care."

"This is our team and yes, we may win, but at the moment we are losing together. There's nothing Coach Sanders or Coach Keller, or even I can do to actually make you care enough to be great. That has to trigger somewhere inside of you."

"And here is the hardest aspect of all of this. That at the end of the season people will tell you good job no matter what we do. Even if we win the state championship, we are expected to do our best next season. It's not about the end of the road; it's about how you travel the road. The sun will come up after a loss or a win. It is simply knowing that you have chosen the path of greatness." Both assistant coaches were nodding their heads in agreement. The team was silent. Coach Reiner couldn't tell if his words were making a difference or not; the boys were stoned faced.

"Right now, I don't think you care. In fact, practice is over. I don't want to see any of you tomorrow unless you care enough to be something different. That you want to start a winning tradition, and you actually want to be a champion." The team flinched. A murmur started but Coach Reiner's voice cut it short.

"And I don't mean a champion by simply winning games, but that you live every single day on the right path. The path that means that you are striving to be excellent." Coach Reiner paused, blew his whistle, and then said, "Practice is over. If you care enough, I'll see you tomorrow."

Coach Reiner turned, grabbed a water bottle, and walked off the field. Coach Sanders and Coach Keller looked at each other for a second. They hollered at Sam to get the gear together and walked off the field, too. The team sat there wondering what to do next.

A few freshmen started to horse around. Jason stood up and said, "Knock it off! I don't know about you guys, but winning is a heckuva lot more fun than losing. And I do care enough to make this football program something more. I'll see you guys tomorrow." Jason grabbed his helmet and walked off the field.

Teon, Troy, Kyle and a few of the other seniors stood up and walked off, too. As the seniors started, then the rest of the team followed, however, Mike stayed behind. He sat on the bench just enjoying the afternoon sunshine. He let his mind wander over different topics. One of the thoughts centered on what Coach Reiner said. Mike wondered how being great changed anything.

David was feeling agitated. Julie was trying to make him feel better. She was asking questions. But Coach Reiner's mood wasn't getting any better. "Well, do you think the team can bounce back?" Julie asked.

"I don't know." David stood up to refill his glass.

"I was just asking. You don't have to get snippy with me."

It was one of those moments in married life where the attitudes of the couples were miles apart. Julie had actually been having a good week. The fourth-graders were a joy this year. Even Tanner, her one difficult child, made the days fun with his quirky behavior. Today he had told Julie that he knew unicorns were real. They just hid their horn around other horses.

Coach Reiner was not having such a good week. He was proud to see that the football team had returned to practice. But practice really wasn't any better. The team was more focused to a degree; things just weren't working well. He didn't know how to fix it. At the moment he felt like everything he was striving for was about to fall off a cliff. He knew that if they played the way they were practicing, they would have their third loss, and it would not be pretty.

On top of that he understood that his wife didn't deserve his negative vibe, however, he also couldn't help but be snippy.

"I'm sorry. I didn't mean to be. Things are just not be going well."

"Sometimes you don't have to bring football into the house."

Coach Reiner slammed the fridge door. "At this moment football is the most important thing. I do need to bring it home. If only to have a safe place to process and work through some of the issues."

There was a heavy silence. Julie said, "Dinner is ready."

They ate in silence for a couple of minutes. Coach Reiner sighed deeply inside. "How are the fourth graders doing?"

Julie wasn't in the mood now for small talk. She could be pretty bullheaded when she was in a testy mood. "Fine."

Coach Reiner rubbed his brow over the bridge of his nose. The moment felt just like practice, he and Julie were just not clicking.

"Does the new math program seem to be helping?" Coach Reiner was trying to bridge the emotional gap he created. These moments never cross people's minds when they date. When you're dating, it's easy to go your own way to take a breather when things are rough. But when you are married there was no place to actually go beside separate rooms. Julie decided that was probably a good option. She got up, cleaned her plate, and put it in the dishwasher. Coach Reiner audibly sighed.

Questions started to create frustration in David's mind. Why does it have to be this hard? Why doesn't it just work? He asked, "Okay, what's wrong?"

Julie responded, "Nothing, hon. I'm just done eating. I'm going to get some homework graded." She walked into the bedroom.

David sat at the table picking at his food. He didn't know if he should go in to into the bedroom and try to make things better, or to just give her space. He got up from the table, but then he thought better of it. He would probably just continue to agitate her.

David cleaned off his plate. He decided that he needed to be outside. He grabbed his clipboard off the kitchen counter and went to sit on the stoop.

He turned on the outside lights as the sun was just edging off the horizon. The colors were stark, a sharp red fading to orange with the sky overhead fading into black. Instead of working on some plays he had in his head, he leaned back to watch the stars appear in the sky.

In college, for one of his science credits, David took astronomy. The college had an observatory and for one class period the class met at three in the morning. The telescopes were set to see the planets or constellations. The students showed up groggy and grumpy but within a couple minutes of observing the night sky their attitude changed to amazement.

Coach Reiner loved observing the constellations. Instead of making him feel small, he somehow felt everything was all right. That things were in order. He felt at ease when he got the chance to just sit and look at the night sky.

Ten minutes later he heard the door open. Julie came without a word and sat next to him. She leaned back and took in the brilliance of the stars. One of their first dates was to the observatory at the college. Julie knew that David enjoyed the night sky.

Neither one of them said anything but David reached out to grasp his wife's hand as they sat on the porch.

Coach Keller was enjoying a cup of coffee at Sandy's Diner. It was Wednesday night. The night when most of the old guard sat to discuss life. The conversation turned to football and Coach Reiner. Most of the conversation was about how the boys were not playing up to their potential. Even with Coach Keller there, the men expressed their opinions openly.

Russ straight up asked Coach Keller why he had not taken the head coaching position last year. "Your defense usually plays pretty good. You seem to have a good vibe with the boys."

Coach Keller knew that in small towns the men would always talk about football, and that most of the time, they didn't mean much harm. "Just don't want to be talked about all the time here at Sandy's

I guess," Coach Keller said with a smile. The group of guys laughed. Coach Keller said, "I think you need to give Coach Reiner a little bit more credit than you do. It's amazing how fast you forget that before he took the job, wins were really sparse. And last year we had four wins."

"Agreed, but he's starting 0 and 2 again. He doesn't get his team going right away," said Joe Adams, one of the pharmacists in town.

"Well, I think you also forgot how close the first game actually was. The fourth down." The men all nodded in agreement. They started to complain about how hard it was to win on that field. How the refs always favored the Haymakers. How the Vikings never got a call. Coach Keller chuckled to himself

The old crew came to a consensus that Coach Reiner still needed time with the boys. Programs take time to develop. Coach Keller dropped few bits of knowledge into the conversation but for most part just enjoyed the atmosphere. Coach Keller was, in his own right, an "Old Boy." He had been at Twin Valley for 12 years. He enjoyed the community and the way football was an underlying thread for everyone. Wednesday nights at Sandy's tied everyone together.

Coach Keller knew that he needed to get home soon to finalize some defensive blitz packages. This third game was a must win because a program only gets so much time.

Coach Keller paid his bill and said good night to the boys. As he was heading out he ran into, Dan, Jason's dad. Dan reached out to shake Coach Keller's hand telling him to keep up the good work. As he was heading out the door he could hear the old boys greet Dan in unison.

Coach Keller actually kind of hated to leave, but he knew he had work to do.

Coach Sanders sat at his kitchen table. He was already working on the playbook for basketball season. His wife, Rachel, came in.

"Hon, are you working on basketball already?" She was an understanding woman. She actually didn't like sports at all but enjoyed the conversations and the community aspect of going to basketball games with soup suppers. She always found a way to help out, even at opposing teams' gyms. "Football season isn't even over yet, dear."

"I know. But I just wanted to get ahead a little bit."

She bent down and kissed him on the cheek. "I'm going to get some laundry and then start on my new book."

"Okay, I think I'll be done in a little while."

More as an afterthought she asked, "How do you think the team is doing?"

Coach Sanders stopped sketching out a play to think for a moment. "Last game was a disaster, that's for sure. I really think that the players are starting to see what it takes. I'm actually really excited about the upcoming basketball season. I think we'll get the football team back playing to the level that they should be. And I think that will carry over to basketball. I think we can win the district title this year."

"Really? You guys did a good job last season. I think you've got them going in the right direction."

"Yeah, it takes some time. The athletes here definitely have the talent more so than Hillcrest. But talent isn't enough. We did a lot with hard work at Hillcrest. If these boys did that kind of work…" Coach paused, "I see a state title."

"Maybe. What I do know is that the community is enjoying the change in fortunes of the teams. I was at the hair salon and even the ladies were talking about the football team."

Coach Sanders chuckled, "We have made it big time if the ladies at the hair salon are talking about us."

"I am just saying that what you guys have been doing is being noticed."

Coach Sanders understood. This was actually his third job. He started coaching at a small school right out of college. He only had eight kids out for basketball his first year. His second job, Hillcrest, was a great experience. The team had made it to state the last three years, mostly on work ethic. It was a tough decision to leave, but Twin Valley was a class level higher. Coach Sanders played with the idea of making it to the collegiate level. He didn't know if he would get the chance to make it to that level, but making the jump up in class gave him a better chance.

"I know. It'll be exciting that's for sure. I'm not going to lie, I am excited to get basketball started, but I'm just as excited to see what we can do with football."

"Can't wait to see you on the court." His wife stood up and

wrapped her arms around her husband. “I'm proud of you.” She planted a serious kiss on his lips. “Don't stay up too late with your basketball plays.” Rachel went downstairs to do laundry.

Coach Sanders returned to his rough draft of his playbook on the table. He wasn’t actually too worried about the football team. He believed in the same basic philosophies of Coach Reiner. He didn't always agree with his discipline style, but they matched on a lot of key points of athletic development.

His mind quickly turned back to a transition offense. He would put his work away after midnight.

“Coach?” asked Sam.

“What, Sam?” Coach Reiner asked back.

“We forgot the kicking tees.” Sam was a senior. He had been the student manger since sixth grade. He enjoyed the small aspects of the job, setting up the athletic tapes in small pyramids in the training room, watching film with Coach and marking down the notes as Coach Reiner asked. He took pride in the things that made the football team run smoothly behind the scenes. The last two years had been the best so far. Coach Reiner appreciated the small things. He would bring Sam a Code Red Mountain Dew for film sessions. Coach always told him thank you. Sam felt horrible, then felt even worse as Coach's right hand started to rub and pinch the top bridge of his nose. That meant he was trying to control his frustration.

"What should I do?" Sam asked.

Coach Reiner couldn't even think. The bus was late because of a mix up with the drivers. They had a horrible week of practice after the debacle at North Star Catholic to go to 0 and 2. And to top it off this team, the Patriots, had ended the Vikings' season last year with a loss.

"I'll get it solved," Coach Reiner said.

Sam was discouraged. He left to get the water bottles ready.

Coach Reiner walked across the field. The teams were running through their position drills. "Kevin, catch and secure." Coach demonstrated with his hands. Hands out to catch an imaginary ball, then moved his right hand to his chest to secure the imaginary ball. Kevin nodded his head. He secured the ball high and tight as he ran back to the receiver line. Coach Reiner continued across the field to find Coach Johnson.

They shook hands and made small talk. The Patriots were 1-

1. Coach Johnson had been at the school for eight years. The team had been to the play-offs off and on four times. Last year both teams ended their season 4-5, but the Patriots ended the season with a win and the Vikings a loss. The Patriots reflected the same attitude of their coach, a mix of simple respect but with a condescending edge. Even if they lost they would demonstrate an air of superiority. Coach Johnson smiled in that way when Coach Reiner asked if they had an extra three-point tee they could use during the game.

Coach Reiner thanked him and returned to the Vikings' sideline. He handed the tee, with one of the ends secured by athletic tape, to Sam. "Please, return this to them when the game is over."

"OK, sorry, Coach."

"Don't let it happen again," Coach Reiner said as he patted Sam on the shoulder.

"I won't." Sam returned to setting up the equipment on the bench. Sam had a system, one bench for injuries. This bench had all the med kits, with a few things out and ready, like tape and tape scissors. One bench for "meetings," single player or team. Clipboards, markers, and the small water bottle container. The third bench was his "game" bench. This bench had the coolers, a box with snack bags filled with dried fruit and granola, a bag with mints for Coach Keller, and Sam's bottle of Code Red. It also held the ball bag, tees, and the equipment box to handle those small moments, like a busted chinstrap. Sam was working on the first bench.

Coach Reiner rubbed the bridge of his nose, and moved to rubbing his forehead right above his brow. He thought to himself, *we have to win this game; we have to win this game.* Four minutes to kick-off.

As luck would have it, the Vikings lost the coin toss and got to use the borrowed tee to start the game. The Patriots returned the kick to the 35-yard line, and then proceeded to march the ball down the field. Their linemen were opening holes wherever they wished. Sweep right, 8 yards. Belly dive, six yards. Counter trap, twelve yards. Coach Keller looked over at Coach Reiner with a frown. "This could be a long game," Coach Keller whispered.

As the Patriots gained seven yards on a fullback trap crossing the Vikings' 30-yard line, Coach Reiner felt everything weighing on his shoulders. The promise that if they worked hard they would succeed. And the boys *had* worked hard. If they would have just won that first game… The Patriots picked up another four yards.

Why was it was so hard to change failure? The team had the

talent, no question. Coach Reiner knew he was still learning to be a head coach. Everything felt like it was falling into place in August. The Patriots were at the Vikings' 22-yard line.

Coach Reiner rubbed the bridge of his nose. The Patriots ran another counter trap and moved the ball to the Vikings 16 yard line. Coach Keller was starting to send in the defensive play, but Coach Reiner grabbed his hands stopping him. Coach Reiner had enough; he called a timeout.

"Eyes on me!" The Vikings turned from their huddle, even a few Patriots players turned. Coach Reiner's voice wasn't loud, but it was angry and shot across the field.

"I'm not sure what you think you're doing, but if they score, you are all done for the night!" You could see the Patriot players respond to Coach Reiner's words. You could almost see them laugh. Coach Reiner didn't even see them; he was focused on his words and his team. "This is not who we are. This is not what we stand for. This is not how we practice. This is not how champions play. You have a play or two to show me that this team cares enough to do it better." Coach Reiner's emotions got the best of him. He threw down his headset. "I expect greatness from you, and you play like this. This is crap! Decide who you are! Coach Keller, set your defense." Coach Reiner started to walk away, trying to gather up his headset, then turned back and said, "They score, you are all done." It seemed the whole stadium was watching their sideline now.

Coach Reiner was already regretting what he said. *You have to keep your cool*, he thought to himself. *There will always be tough times. You have to keep your head to get through it.* Coach Reiner's inner voice was running wild in his head. How was he going to handle the defense if they did score? The game was far from over, but he had made a challenge to them and would now have to follow through. Coach Reiner looked at his clipboard for answers. The marker board only held an empty field.

The Vikings set their defense without a word. Coach Reiner almost couldn't watch. He couldn't tell if his words did any good.

The Patriots broke their huddle. The quarterback smiled at Coach Reiner and gave him a head bob, as if to say "get your subs ready for defense." Jason saw him.

Coach Keller had set a line stunt to the left with a Sam, strong side linebacker, blitz. Coach Keller was guessing on a strong side play. Jason would cut across the guard's nose to hit the A gap.

Troy, the Sam linebacker, would stunt hard one yard outside of the tight end. In a way they were selling out for a play to the right.

The team knew Coach Reiner was serious. Rarely did he lose it to throw his head set. Jason set his hand down. He was tired of the lackluster attitude from the team and more importantly from himself. He didn't know if the team would follow suit, but he didn't like the idea of losing another game. His dad didn't raise him that way. Jason had made his choice, and he hoped the team had made the same choice.

Teon, at first, was angry at Coach's words. He about decided to just let the receiver go, no matter what the play might be. He didn't need to be put down in front of everybody like that. But Coach's words ran through his mind again... "Decide who you are..." and the meaning clicked for him. He thought to himself. "I want to be great."

Troy didn't get the meaning of Coach Reiner's outburst. He was pissed off. All he heard was "you play like crap" and it set him off. He thought to himself, *I'll show him.*

The Patriot's quarterback started his cadence. "Red 12, Red 12... Set. Hut!"

Jason didn't wait to see if it was on two. He took a small step left with his left foot. He threw his right arm up and into the guard as he drove his right leg across his midline. He followed that with a quick left step, and he was through the A gap. The Patriots were running to their right, a speed option play. Jason saw the quarterback turning to his right as the halfback moved in unison with him. Jason focused in on the red number 7, setting his arms by his side to piston out and wrap the quarterback up. He just missed pinning the quarterback's right arm as it shot out, getting the ball pitched toward the halfback. Jason didn't see where the ball went, as he made sure the quarterback felt the impact of the ground.

Troy made a mistake in his assignment; he was to go outside one yard. His job was to keep the play inside. But he was so mad that he bit on the halfback's first steps to the right, another mistake. As a linebacker he was to read the guard's helmet first, then the backfield. As Coach Keller liked to say, "Don't trust running backs, trust the guard." But Troy was playing on emotion; he just wanted to hit somebody. After the running back's first step Troy decided he was going to hit the running back squarely between the numbers. He made a beeline through the C gap.

Coach Reiner watched. The voice in his head was quiet for the moment. He was ready to call the second team defense into the game. He needed to follow through with his words, or he would never have the team's trust. If he didn't mean what he just said, they could not trust he meant anything he ever said, even when he praised them.

As the ball was snapped, Coach Reiner thought to himself, *Wow, what a great first step by Jason.* He saw the Patriots' quarterback pitch the ball as Jason wrapped him up, and started to cuss in his head as he saw the line Troy had taken to the back. In Troy's intensity, he had made a third error, he aimed for where the back was, not where he would be in the next step. The best Troy would be able to do is turn and hope to grab jersey as the running back sprinted past him. Then it seemed time stood still.

Troy's instincts told him he was going to miss the halfback so he started to stand up in his form so he could turn, when something flashed in front of him. Without thinking, even startled a little, he grabbed the blur in front of him. It was the ball.

Later, Coach Reiner would swear that Troy stopped cold in his pursuit of the running back to look at the ball in his hands. Troy would say he knew he could catch the pitch and planned to run it back for the touchdown at the snap of the ball. Troy's smile would broaden though as he confessed on the bus ride home that the ball did seem to come out of nowhere.

Whatever the case, Troy continued forward and was in a dead sprint for the end zone before anyone on either team knew what happened. Teon sprinted by Coach Reiner on the sideline, as the team headed down the field to get ready for the extra point and said, "Coach, how's that for greatness?" Coach Reiner answered with a high-five as Teon passed by.

Coach Reiner turned toward the crowd when he heard a shout of pride, "That's my boy! That's my boy!" Charlie was on the fence line. The fans around him were celebrating with him. Coach Reiner couldn't help but think what a crazy strong bond there was between fathers and sons. How each of them lifted or tore down each other's sense of purpose in this life. A son's shining moment reflected in a father's heart. How a father's words weighed heavy in a son's reflection of himself. Coach Reiner smiled for both Troy and Charlie, because Coach Reiner also knew how fractured the bond was for some.

The Vikings would use the borrowed tee for three more touchdowns. The final score was 28-3 Vikings. Coach Reiner returned the tee himself, making sure he said thank you.

Troy walked into the house. Not totally sure what to expect since he saw that there were lights on. Both his mom and dad were sitting in the living room. They didn't seem to be talking, but they weren't fighting either.

Troy knew that his dad had been at the game, Charlie was at every game. In fact he heard him throughout the game. But Troy hadn't seen his mom there. But as he walked in she stood up and wrapped her arms around him. "What an exciting game, son!"

Troy hugged his mom back feeling a little awkward due to the sudden expression of affection from his mom.

"What a game, son. I am so proud. It reminded me of my last game of my senior year." Charlie started in.

Troy might have given away his feelings about listening to his dad break into another story. But Charlie stopped the story and sat back down to ask his son questions about the game.

Troy at first felt uncomfortable with the new attention his parents were giving him. It felt so good to have their full attention that he was soon lost his discomfort and talked about the game. Troy felt the most pride when he saw his dad's reaction as Troy talked about his defensive touchdown play.

"I'll be honest. I have never seen a defensive play like that intercepted pitch," Charlie said, excited about recounting the play that changed the momentum of the game. "Tell the truth, son, did you plan to get their pitch when you blitzed?"

"Well, yeah, of course I did." Troy smiled and then confessed to being ticked off at Coach Reiner. "I was so angry that I just went on the snap of the ball. As I read the halfback, I was just trying to hit him, and the ball appeared in front of me. And then I just took off."

Charlie had a shadow of disappointment across his face but he quickly changed that. "But you did catch it, and you, and you're so fast that nobody even moved. You had that ball so quick. You should've seen the opposing coach. He threw down his clipboard and everything."

His mom spoke up, "I couldn't hear exactly what Coach Reiner said, but I thought I heard him call you guys crap."

"No, mom. I mean yeah, he said we were playing like that."

His mom added, "That's not right for a coach to do that."

Charlie broke into the conversation; "Actually, what he said was right, you guys started the game like shit. Our coaches used to yell and holler at us. I heard Coach Reiner calling you guys out a little bit. Coach Burn used to tell us what slime bags we were."

Troy didn't say anything. He just let his dad talk for a little bit. After the play, it had clicked for Troy what Coach was actually trying to say to them. He understood that Coach Reiner believed in them and that they were simply playing to a level that was unacceptable.

The family stayed up for another 45 minutes talking about the game and other things. Both of them told Troy that he probably should get some rest. They knew that he had weights in the morning with film review. Troy agreed even though he was enjoying the attention from his parents and didn't want it to end.

They both had plans of going out. It was their normal routine. Troy smiled though when he noticed that his mom and dad were going out together. Maybe for the first time in a long time and he could live with that.

8 GAME FOUR

Kids were mulling around the street. The noise and excitement was a blanket filling the downtown square. The community pep rally was actually a cool idea, thought Coach Reiner. He was also glad it was held Friday afternoon. It allowed the team to get back into a normal routine at the end of the day.

Troy was dressed in his game jersey and jeans, as were the rest of the team. He was headed toward the football players as they found seats on the makeshift stage. Troy walked past the cheerleaders setting up in front of the stage. Ashley smiled at him.

She was a sophomore, and she was on the edge of beautiful. She had an innocent way she carried herself. Her smile was simple and her eyes were naturally blue and striking, hinting at the woman she would become.

Troy knew who she was but rarely crossed paths with her in school or in social ways. But for whatever reason, maybe it was the way she smiled at him over her pom-poms that made Troy pay attention to her today. He glanced at her again. Troy watched her interact with the other cheerleaders. Somehow the crowd around her blurred, but Ashley's body stood out, features sharp. Troy's mind started to race. He couldn't shake reality back into focus. Ashley turned to see if Troy was looking at her, and her faced beamed when their eyes met. Troy tried to start a conversation with George sitting next to him, but he found he could not last more than a few minutes without looking at Ashley.

Coach Reiner made his way to the makeshift podium to give a small speech. He looked out over the crowd. The elementary kids were sitting crossed legged or on their knees with their feet underneath them. Their faces filled with excitement to be outside. Coach Reiner felt a tinge of jealousy. Many of these kids would be at the game tonight. The boys would be involved in their own game of football beside the concession stand. Not caring about watching, but playing. The plays drawn on palms or on the ground. The girls would be congregated on the fence, imitating the cheerleaders, excited to follow the routines. The kids believed in the joy of the game, the joy of cheering.

Coach Reiner let his eyes flow over the crowd. The junior high kids were putting on a show, believing the whole world was watching them. Boys pushing and shoving each other, girls swinging their hair, or laughing too loud. His eyes found the old boy network, never a smile but always an opinion. Then there were the parents, cameras out, taking pictures of everything. His team was to his left, some of them acting out for their moms with the cameras.

"I know we are not quite where we wanted to be at this time of the year. But tonight's game will give us a chance to be .500 early in the season. The freshmen up to the seniors have been a great group of boys," said Coach Reiner.

Coach Reiner looked towards the chairs where the seniors were sitting. He smiled at them, and then he said, "This is your senior class. I cannot ask for a better bunch of boys to be a part of the team. Tonight will be your last Homecoming game. Make it count. Play like champions." The cheerleaders raised their pom-poms to start a cheer. Ashley smiled at Troy again, then went back to cheering. Troy couldn't keep his eyes off of her.

Ashley was infatuated with Troy. She watched his number on the football field and day dream about kissing him. She only knew him by his persona on the football field and in the hallways. But he had captured her eye.

Coach Reiner was continuing his speech, "I am very thankful for all your support this season, and I hope that you enjoy our victory tonight." The crowd erupted and the band started to play the school fight song.

Troy ran to catch Ashley at the end of the pep rally. "Are you going to the game?" There was an awkward pause as Troy figured out what he had just asked. He tried to laugh it off.

"Yes, I'll be there cheering like I have every Friday night." Troy smiled. Teon hollered at him that they were heading back to the school.

Troy said, "I... I'll... I'll see you tonight then." And headed off with the team.

Teon punched Troy in the shoulder. "I saw you talking to … What's her name?"

Troy said, "Ashley. You know, I was just… talking to her."

Teon said, "Oh I know, dog. I know you're a smooth

criminal."

Troy smiled, yet he couldn't explain how fast this feeling had hit. Crazy how love could strike at any moment in your life. Football was the furthest thing from Troy's mind.

Coach Reiner sat in his office nervously looking at the first ten scripted plays. He knew that they should win this game. They had soundly beaten the Eagles last year. The Eagles looked better on film this year, but the Vikings had more talent. This would be a good morale booster to win Homecoming and to get to their second win of the season. Yet the butterflies kicked in just like they did every game.

Coach Reiner stepped into the locker room. The boys were finishing taping ankles and putting on gear. He went over to the radio to turn it down. "OK guys, we have about fifteen minutes before we need to head out for special teams' warm-ups. I know this is an exciting time. But you have to let Homecoming go and concentrate on football."

Troy was thinking about Ashley. He kept telling himself that he had to start thinking about the game, but it wasn't working. He was imagining running out to the field and seeing her on the sidelines smiling at him.

Coach Reiner continued, "We should win this game. You know that I'm honest with you. But we can we can lose this game if we lose our focus. So we need to work on the basics and get this win."

Coach Keller said, "On the defensive end we need to contain number 12 and number 27. The read option is best when the defense makes a mistake. Do your job and trust everyone else will do theirs."

"All right, everybody, grab a teammate's hand," Coach Reiner said. "This is our team. We may win, or we may lose. But we will do it together. This is our moment. This is our time. This is Viking football." Coach Reiner stood up, "This is game time!" The team erupted and headed out to the field.

Coach Reiner's patience was tried on the first play of the game. The Vikings won the coin toss and deferred to the second half. Kale kicked the ball down to the five-yard line, but the Eagles ran the kickoff back to the Vikings' 10-yard line. And with one play from the line of scrimmage, they scored. To add to his frustration, the Eagles converted on their two-point attempt. This was going to be a long game.

The Vikings answered back with a 10-play drive that ended in a field goal. Then the defenses took over. At halftime the score was still eight to three. Coach Reiner wasn't happy.

"Troy, it's like you don't have your head in the game. We have to execute if we even hope to have a chance at winning this game. They came to play. Did you?" Coach Reiner pointed his finger at Troy. "Did you? *Did you*?" He continued to ask each senior the same question. "We need some more energy out of you. We need you to play to win."

The team played better in the second half. They still couldn't get their offense rolling against the Eagle's defense. The Eagle defense was playing error free. Every player was doing their job. The Vikings' receivers never seemed to be open, and they never gained more than five yards on a run

There were four minutes left in the fourth quarter. The score still stood 8 to 3. Mike looked around at his teammates, they looked confident but were showing signs of fatigue. They were leaning over, hands on their thigh pads or lifting their eyes to the sky and breathing in heavy sighs. Mike had done a better job in the second half leading the team. He knew that this might be their last chance at a scoring drive. Troy had been running better, but the Eagle's defense seemed to focus in on him.

"OK guys, we've got to do this." Mike said. The team murmured in agreement. "Let's get to the end zone and put these guys away!"

Thoughts of Ashley had distracted Troy during the first half, but Troy was able to put thoughts of her away in the second half. Football was his main focus. Getting lost in the game and playing on instinct was what he was doing now.

The Vikings started their drive on their own 32-yard line. They chipped away at the defense; three yards here, two yards there. Mike tried twice to get shots downfield, but the Eagles' defense was ready for that. One pass was knocked down. The second one was too far out of bounds for Teon to grab. The Eagles would not break.

By chipping away at the defense they kept the drive going, but they used up too much clock. The Vikings found themselves on the Eagles' 38-yard line with one minute and 58 seconds to go. Coach Reiner called a timeout. He had one left.

“Guys, this is our last two minutes. A field goal will not win this game. We have to score a touchdown.”

The team looked and felt exhausted. The grind it out football was wearing on them mentally. The whole week of Homecoming activities, the anticipation of the dance, and just creating a winning attitude was wearing on them. Coach Reiner could see it in the way they walked back to the huddle, so he had decided to call a time out to get them focused.

“I think you know the importance of this game. We cannot go one and three. We need to get this win to be .500,” Coach Reiner paused for effect. “This is one of those moments. A moment that defines a game, a season. That is why I love this game. For these moments. These are our testing grounds. To see if we are champions. I promise you, this victory will feel awesome because you fought for it.”

The team looked at each other. This is what coach had been preaching about, grabbing the moment. Actually succeeding on their own merits. Playing championship football.

“We only have one timeout left, so we are going to have to pass a little bit more. They're setting the strong safety on you, Mike.

He's been moving to your side, following your head, where you look."

Mike said, "I know, Coach, but I don't have time to get to the second read."

"We'll make time for you." Kyle said. The rest of the linemen agreed.

Coach Reiner liked the attitude but did not feel the confidence coming from the team. At times like this is when a team and individuals were tested. Many people talk about being great, but very few actually come through with doing what they say. This was the one difference between being great and being average. Actually doing what you say you'll do. Kyle had set the bar for the team.

"Okay we're going to pass on this first down Houston Zip 7-3-5, and then we're going to run an Indy 27 trap on the second play. After that we'll see what has happened. Look for the call from the sideline."

The team huddled up to repeat the plays. Mike reminded them that they would get to the line for the second play. Troy couldn't gauge how the team felt. They were all tired, but exhaustion had a way of focusing you. To focus your mind to where the moment was what was most important. The team was at that point, where they were too tired to actually worry about anything else than what needed to be done.

"Red 27, red 27. Set... Hut!" Mike took his five-step drop.

Mike did have time. He saw Randy cutting across the middle on the second read. The strong safety had followed Mike's eyes following Teon on the out route and had over played, leaving the middle open. Mike delivered a 12-yard pass to Randy.

The Vikings got straight to the line setting up in the pro formation. Mike called out his cadence. He turned and quickly handed the ball to the fullback, Brock. The clock was counting down one minute 24 seconds, one minute 23 seconds, one minute 22 seconds.

The Eagles defense crashed hard, filling the gaps to stop Brock for no gain. They were on the Eagles' 26-yard line. Coach Reiner had to make a quick decision. He decided to call his last timeout. It was second and ten with one minute 20 seconds on the clock.

The team gathered around Coach Reiner, including Coach Keller and Coach Sanders. Coach Reiner stood and looked at the clock for a second and then another second and then another. He turned towards his team. "These are the moments we play for. These are the moments that define us. All your practice time, all the time in the weight room. All that time spent so that you could be here with the opportunity to be great with one minute and 20 seconds."

The team looked at him with renewed energy. They understood.

"Let's go Viking Left Set A." This would set the three receivers on the left side and two receivers on the right. Teon would be on the right sideline headed toward the end zone. Mike flashed back to the first game. He took a breath, thought how ironic life could be, to be in a similar situation three weeks later. He had failed once; he wasn't going to fail again.

Coach Reiner continued, "We can win it on this play, but we still have enough time if it's incomplete. If we hit Randy underneath, you need to get to the line and spike the ball to stop the clock. Be ready to get the call from me. We don't have anymore time outs."

The team felt ready. They had enough time. They knew the game was in their hands. Victory or defeat was their responsibility. The team huddled up ready for Mike to repeat the plays. He looked at all of them and said, "This is our team. We may win or we may lose, but we do this together." Football was a game of emotions, and Mike was trying to tap into his team's reserves.

The Eagles' defense stayed in their four-four but spread out to match the Vikings' formation. Mike knew he would probably get pressure on the outside. He prepared himself to feel the pressure. He took a deep breath, and told himself to stay calm and just play.

"Green 72, green 72, set... Hut!"

The snap was perfect. Mike set his feet. The Eagles had decided to go all out on the play also. They sent the middle linebacker behind a line twist with the defensive left tackle. Jason had control of his man, but Kyle didn't see the blitz in time. Kyle shuffled his feet first, turning his body, too. He was too late. Kyle was only able to chip the linebacker on the shoulder as he busted through the line.

Mike was using Randy's route for his first read. Hoping that Teon would be one-on-one on his sideline route. Because Randy's route was coming across the middle, Troy saw number 52 come through the line. His instincts as a quarterback took over. The thousands of reps to hold his ground in the pocket. Using hand dummies to create pressure. Building the automatic timing in his reaction. Suppressing the urge to run or bail right away on a play. To trick the defense. Mike tried to see the field; Randy was almost even with him. To seem calm in the pocket, while his body itched to make its move.

The defensive end, number 52, was aiming for Mike's back shoulder. This line of attack was taught to keep QBs from going outside on a pass rush. Mike knew this as he made his move. His first step was actually at the linebacker with his left foot. Mike could see number 52's eyes. With his left foot planted, Mike pushed hard to his right, just as the defensive end was ready to wrap up. Troy made a good move, but had to shake his shoulders hard to release the defender's hand that was able to grab jersey as he went past. Troy reset his feet.

Mike quickly glanced at Randy's route. Randy had sat on his route and was still open in the middle of the field. The clock in his head was blaring; it told him he had passed the four second mark. He felt pressure from his right side. He saw Teon five yards out of the end zone. The clock in his head told him he was late. Randy was the safe pass; they would still have time to get another play off. But he wanted what all athletes want, another chance to prove themselves. He threw the ball towards the back pylon.

What Mike didn't see was that the free safety was sitting in the end zone. That was why Randy's route was open. As the ball was released the free safety sprinted towards the corner. The cornerback had good coverage on Teon. All three of them, plus the ball, were on course to meet in the back of the end zone.

The ball was actually a little short this time. Mike had taken a hit as he released the ball and was laying facedown in the grass getting irritated as the defender seemed to just lay on top of him. Mike positioned himself in the pushup position and angrily shed the defender from his back while trying to watch the ball. Teon read the arc of the ball and started to slow down. The free safety was tracking the ball like a centerfielder. Noticing Teon's eyes, the corner had turned his head to find the ball as he ran beside Teon.

Coach Reiner watched from the sideline. His worst thoughts played out on the field. It looked like the free safety would be able to intercept the ball. The Vikings wouldn't even have a chance at another play. The ball started its arc downward. The cornerback started to slow down to make a play on the ball. Both Eagles' defenders jumped, hands extended into the air. It looked like the free safety, number 10, would come down with the ball. Teon had waited a half second before he jumped. His hands came through the defenders hands snagging the ball from the free safety. Teon brought the ball back onto his chest as he fell to the ground. He landed and bounced. Air escaped his chest. In a panic he tried to find the ref to see the signal. His lungs were trying to get air back into him, but his heart wanted to know the signal. He spotted the ref to his left. The referee's hands went up to signal a touchdown. The home crowd erupted. Teon fought for his breath.

Coach Sanders jumped almost as high as Teon did. On the sideline, the team turned and high-fived each other. Coach Reiner was calling out for the two-point conversion when he saw Troy motioning to him to come to Teon's side. Coach Reiner heard a whistle as he ran to the end zone. He could see Teon was panicking. "Calm down, Teon. You got the wind knocked out of you. Relax." Teon was still holding onto the ball as his breathing came in short, incomplete bursts. "Relax. You're OK." Just like that Teon's chest let go and filled with air.

After a few seconds, Teon let go of the ball and got to his

feet. Everyone clapped as he headed to the sidelines. "Coach Sanders, we need a sub for Teon on the extra point."

Coach Reiner had already decided on the two-point conversion. There was enough time left for the Eagles to kick a field goal. The two-point conversion would give them a three-point lead. If they didn't convert, it would be a one-point lead. The game would be decided by the defense. One minute 10 seconds left.

The Vikings went to the line with a double twin set on each side with a single back. The call was a speed option to the left. The Eagles shut down the play, pushing Troy out of bounds for no gain. Coach Reiner and Coach Keller talked quickly about defensive strategy. Many times a prevent defense gave up too many yards, and a field goal would now win the game for the Eagles. Coach Reiner and Coach Keller both agreed they would play their normal defense.

The kickoff was a touchback. The Eagles would have to march at least 60 yards to have a real chance at winning the game. The Eagles had two timeouts left. On the first play they ran a middle screen. Jason tackled the running back from behind, but it was still an eight-yard gain. The Eagles lined up right after the play on the ball. They had planned to go for the win on the second play.

Sometimes hard lessons have to be learned during the season. The defensive backs were ready for the deep pass. Unlike the first game of the season, they were not going to let anybody get behind them this time. The free safety, Riley, a junior, was playing like a centerfielder. As the ball was heading down the sideline, he gauged the trajectory and snagged it before the receiver could even make a play. Game over. The Vikings were .500 for the first time under Coach Reiner.

Since it was Homecoming, the feeling in the air was electric. The student body rushed the sideline and onto the field as the teams were shaking hands. The Viking coaches tried to keep the students away so that the Eagles could get to the locker room.

Ashley found her way to Troy, "Good game."

"Thanks," Troy said. They stood looking at each other for a few seconds, eyes connecting, energy flowing between them. This was going to be crazy.

"Are you going to the dance?" Troy asked.

"Yes, I am," Ashley said.

Before Troy could ask any more questions the football team grabbed him and rushed him off to the locker room. He looked back and hollered; "I'll see you there." Ashley smiled and headed to talk with the other cheerleaders.

The Homecoming dance was like any high school Homecoming dance. There were groups of girls all dancing freely to the music. There were couples that held each other too tight and a range of people mingling around the wall and by the food. Ashley and Troy danced a few times. During a slow dance Ashley made sure that they were an arm's-length apart. Troy tried gently to move her closer, but she resisted. She said, "Well, we're not dating."

Unexpectedly, this made Ashley even more attractive to Troy. A girl who gently but strongly stood for what she believed. Ashley Lester left the Homecoming dance at 11:30. She left because it was her curfew, and she wasn't going to break it, even though most of the upperclassmen were headed to the elementary gym for the Homecoming festivities. Troy had fun with all his teammates but the scent of Ashley continued to play in his head. He had never truly felt this type of connection before in his life.

9 GAME FIVE

The boys rambled into Coach Reiner's room, backpacks slung against the wall. Chatter filled the room like a fog. It was hard just to get through the room as the boys haphazardly found space to sprawl out on the floor and desks.

Coach Reiner made his way through the maze of feet and elbows. “OK guys, quiet down.” The noise decreased only a little.

Coach Keller was not in the mood, “Coach asked for you to quiet down!” He didn't yell it but delivered it above the ruckus to make sure his point was made. The team quieted down. Over the weekend Coach Keller and Coach Reiner went around and around about how to game plan for the Colts. They were still at odds about the direction, but Coach Reiner finally said that they would follow his idea. Coach Keller wasn't happy about it.

"Thank you, Coach Keller." Coach Keller simply nodded. "As you know the state reworked the districts, and we have a new team this year, the Colts. I've been watching film of them for a while and talking to some of their opponents from last year. They like to air it out. They average over 300 yards a game. They spend most of their time in shotgun. I swear in one game they ran the ball twice."

The players murmured, shaking their heads in amazement.

"They are a different type of team than what we normally face. And I think we have to do something different if we are going to defeat them. Over the weekend Coach Keller and I decided on a game plan..." Coach Reiner was about to tell the team that Coach Keller didn't agree with him. Coach Reiner, at times, felt like a rookie, especially with Coach Keller's knowledge of defense. Sunday night Coach Reiner almost just gave in to Coach Keller's insistence that their base 4-4 defense could stop them. But Coach Reiner finally said no, they were going to go with his idea. At the end of the day he was the head coach and would take the blame. He asked Coach Keller to come up with a few unique blitzes, but they were going to run a 3-4 - 4.

Coach Reiner looked over at Coach Keller then continued,

"It is a little different. I will cover the basics, and Coach Keller has some new blitzes we will need to learn. I'm going to trust that we know our offense and devote more time to defense."

Coach Reiner turned to the white board and drew up Xs and Os setting up the defense in a 3-4-4 look. As he stepped away, the boys straightened up. Jason raised his hand.

"How is this going to work, Coach?"

"Let me show you." Coach arranged the Os into the Colt's favorite formation, a spread one back shotgun. "They are stubborn in their approach. I understand why. The quarterback, Lane Spellman, number 1, has a great arm. Number 17, Adam Wright, is fast. He won the State 100 meters last year."

"That guy was fast." Teon said. Teon had qualified for last year's state track meet in the high jump.

"But number 87, Morgan Wesson, is their best receiver. He never drops a ball." Coach Reiner continued, "But they don't run. Even in the semi-finals last year, they continued to try to pass the ball in the rainstorm. Their best rushing game was 104 yards last year, with 86 of those yards from number 1. This approach," Coach Reiner slapped his hand on the board, "is a risk, yes. But we will do our best to make them run." Coach Reiner turned his attention toward Coach Keller. "You have to trust me."

Most of the senior boys were at The Bend. They had decided to roast hotdogs at The Bend Wednesday night. They gathered around the fire pit. They stuck the hotdogs on sticks they found around the area.

Troy brought out a cooler filled with too many caffeinated drinks like Mountain Dew, Red Bull, and Monster.

Teon had brought a few huge family size bags of chips that you find at Sam's Club. The bags looked about half the size of a TV.

The boys sat for a while just talking and eating half cooked hotdogs. It was one of those things that only teenagers appreciated.

"So do you think this defense is going to work?" Mike asked.

"I don't know. It's kind of different. But if Coach is right, and the Colts don't really run, I can see how it could work," said Teon.

"I don't know. I just can't… I know I've seen it on film but I can't imagine a team not running," Troy said.

"I don't know if the defense matters as long as we do our jobs," Mike continued.

"Well, it sure does feel a lot better being .500 than losing. The beginning of the year was rough," Jason said.

All the boys agreed at that point. And they let football go as a subject. They continued to eat and horseplay. Jason pulled out some fishing poles.

The boys discovered that there was no easy way to clean or cook or even eat carp even though they tried to.

The night was filled with random conversations and makeshift wrestling matches. The boys did take care not to get too serious. Even though Troy almost had Teon in the water at one point.

The boys decided to pack up camp at about 10 o'clock. Troy was tempted to text Ashley, but he knew that he would need to stay on his best behavior with her. Interestingly enough he also *felt* like being on his best behavior with her. As Troy took Kyle back to his house, he couldn't help but feel a deep satisfaction with life.

Things were not perfect at home, but the attitude and tone of the house was softer. His parents hadn't argued in the last week.

Troy even did his best to clean up after himself a little bit more. He hadn't attended the party last Saturday night. Both of his parents were still drinking, however, Troy thought it was a little less than normal.

Jason headed home. He knew that his dad might not be there. He would most likely be at Grandpa's house handling a few things. Things were looking good for the family. The whole family had come together to help each other out. It was hard work, but it was amazing how a winning football team can affect even the smaller things in life.

Mike decided not to head for home right away. He stopped at the local Pump 'n Pantry just to see who was hanging out. He was disappointed to find that it was just a couple of junior high boys who had nothing better to do. As he got back into his car, he stared at them for a minute remembering that he had also spent a lot of time there as a junior high kid just wasting time

He decided to drive around awhile and listen to music. He knew there wouldn't be too many people out on a Wednesday night, but he didn't want to head home yet. The house was just too empty. He noticed that the more success he had a football, the lonelier he felt at home.

Mike had a small rush of anger against his mom. He squashed it quickly knowing that she was doing her best. Then the anger turned towards his dad.

Mike couldn't quite remember what he looked like anymore. He always had a memory of them playing football. He couldn't recall if it was summer or a weekend, but he remembered when he and his dad played a make-believe football game in the backyard. They would take turns being the quarterback, or receiver, or running back. They would decide on the pass play and the down and situation. They even made up different teams almost every down. The brightest moment was when they decided to make it a game-winning play. Mike was the receiver. They were the Nebraska Cornhuskers against Colorado. Of course it had to be for the National Championship in the Orange Bowl. Mike was sent on a Z route, cutting across the backyard. He remembered that he had to stretch out to catch the ball. Mike landed on his stomach with the ball. He looked up to see that he was still a yard short of what they had deemed the end zone, a small bush on the outside of the fence line.

But when he got up his dad was screaming with his hands up, "Touchdown! Touchdown! Nebraska wins the National

Championship. Mike scores on the last play!" Mike got swept up in the emotion expressed by his dad. He spiked the ball and jumped into his dad's arms. It was one of the greatest moments in his young life.

Even winning the last two games didn't feel anything like that victory hug. Mike turned the radio down and decided to head for home.

Coach Reiner's thoughts were correct. At the end of the first-quarter, the score was already 14 to 14. The Colts had scored on their first drive on just three plays. The Vikings came back with their own scoring drive, mostly on the ground. Then the Colts scored again through the air on one play. The defensive scheme did not seem to be working, but the players were overcompensating; they were trying to do other people's jobs. Coach Reiner called a timeout after the Colts got past midfield after the Vikings had scored a touchdown to tie the game.

He gathered the defense. "You guys have to trust the idea. You need to talk more, we have more DBs, we need to talk more. Trust that the other guy is doing their job so you can do yours."

On the opponent's third drive it seemed as if the message didn't get through, the Colts moved the ball in two plays to the 28-yard line.

But then, somehow, it started to click. The team sat in their zones communicating routes. The defensive line got a sack on the next play. On second down the quarterback overthrew a receiver in a bit of frustration. Then the defense struck with a 64-yard interception return for a touchdown. The Vikings first lead of the game, 21 – 14.

The touchdown return rattled the Colts. On their next possession they went three and out. Coach Keller was just waiting for them to start running. The Colts were bullheaded in their formations and philosophy.

Sometimes the best defense is making an offense do something that they don't want to do. But in this case, the Colts kept trying to force their philosophy on the Vikings, and it just wasn't working. The Vikings' defense bent, but it didn't break.

The Colts scored one more touchdown in the second quarter. The Vikings' defense did a good job and actually recorded two more interceptions. The Vikings' ground game ate up a lot of clock. Troy scored a 40-yard touchdown. In the waning seconds of the first half the Vikings intercepted the ball. They returned it to the 22-yard line. With three seconds left they kicked a field goal to go up 31 to 21. Coach Keller mumbled, "I can't believe they're not running the ball."

"I told you, Coach, they are a pass first team."

"Well, Coach Reiner, your defense seems to be working. But man, that kid can pass."

"That field goal at half was big. I think if we continue to take time off the clock and not give up a big play, I believe this game is ours."

"I agree, Coach, I also agree this is the damndest game I've ever seen in all my years of coaching," Coach Keller said as they reached the locker room.

"All right, guys. I told you this team was different than any we've ever seen." The team agreed and started to tell stories of the first half. Coach Reiner let them talk for a minute. Sometimes you just needed to let them get it out of their system before you instructed them.

"All right. All right, I need your attention. We have to be ready to adjust. If they decide that they're going to run the ball, we will get back into our base 4-4. But I don't think they will. I think they're too stubborn to actually change. But we have to be ready."

Coach Keller took over. "You guys are doing a great job on defense. We just have to make sure we keep the receivers in front of us. Middle backer, be ready. I want to add a little more pressure this half." Coach Keller went over a few tweaks on the defense. The team was ready heading out to do their halftime warm-ups.

The Colts did adjust, but not to running the ball, to a more aggressive and potent passing game. They went to flooding one side of the field outnumbering the defense with receivers. The Vikings' defense did a good job of eliminating the deep threat. However, the Colts scored on their first series with underneath routes. The Vikings responded with a solid drive that ended on a fourth and two on the Colt's 32-yard line. The Vikings could not convert their fourth-down attempt. They handed the ball over.

The Colts' offense seemed to work again as they proceeded to advance into the red zone again with no passes over 10 yards. The Colts' approach was working, but they were taking more time off the clock with the underneath routes. As the fourth quarter began, the Vikings' defense held. The Colts threw two incomplete passes on second and third downs. They brought out the field-goal team to tie the game.

Coach Sanders look at Coach Reiner. "Middle block?"

Coach Reiner nodded and Coach Sanders sent the play in. The middle block was designed around Jason and Tanner, a sophomore lineman that weighed 280 but was still learning the game, to block the offensive guard and tackle down and back into the center. Most field goal teams step down toward their center to create a wall. The middle block was designed not to open a hole, but to make space at the line for the third person, Teon, to block the kick in the air.

Both teams set up on the line. Teon kept his attention on the field-goal kicker. He trusted that Jason and Tanner would have the spot open for him. Jason and Tanner set themselves on the outside shoulders of the guard and tackle. On the snap of the ball they drove the offensive line exactly where they wanted to go. The ball snapped back, Jason and Tanner stepped hard into the line, concentrating more on the backward push so that Teon would have an extra yard to step. Teon took two steps forward and jumped with all his might. As he jumped he closed his eyes focusing on reaching for the sky. He felt the ball brush the top of his fingers. He opened his eyes to find a place to land shouting, "I got it!"

It was just enough. The ball ricocheted to the right hitting the field goal post. Teon landed on top of Jason and Tanner, all three smiling as they heard the home crowd erupt signaling the field goal was no good.

The Vikings took advantage of the momentum change. They put together a time-consuming 12-play drive that ended with a touchdown. 38 to 28. That sealed the game. The Colts scored another touchdown with three seconds left in the game. The Vikings recovered the onside kick as the clock ran out. The Vikings were three and two for the first time in years.

They sat across each other with pepperoni pizza between them. Troy couldn't stop smiling. He couldn't quite look at Ashley for more than a couple seconds, afraid that he'd get lost in her eyes.

Ashley sat comfortably on her side of the table. Her hand sat on her lap. She smiled and laughed when Troy made a joke, otherwise she was quiet. Troy didn't know exactly how to handle the quietness, so he tried to fill the space with all kinds of stories.

"So what's it like being a cheerleader?"

"I don't know. It's fun to energizer crowd, to be a part of the game without like getting hit."

Troy laughed, "Yeah, I can see where getting hit would not be any fun. I mean pom poms do not give any protection."

"No, no, they don't. Why do you like playing football?"

"I don't know. It's a chance to be aggressive. A chance to accomplish something against an opponent. To see what I am made of."

Troy watched Ashley as she lifted the pizza to take a bite. Then the silence was interrupted by his ring tone for a text message. Troy quickly reached into his pocket to silence it.

"It's okay. You can answer it." Ashley said.

Troy quickly checked the message. The boys wanted to know what he was doing. He ignored the message, put his phone on silent and turned his attention back to Ashley. Troy couldn't believe that he felt so much like a junior high kid at the moment. He could almost make up a bad love poem in his head right then and there.

Troy chomped on his pizza taking two big bites in a row, then tried to talk. Ashley lifted an eyebrow to indicate that he didn't need to have a conversation while he ate.

"You know, I don't see you at any parties or anything. Do you not like parties?" Troy asked.

Ashley sat for a moment thinking on how to answer that question. She knew Troy's reputation. But she didn't think that he was such a bad person. In fact, she found him quite cute. "I don't know. Parties are all right. I just find other things to do."

"Like what?" Troy asked.

"Oh, I read. My friends come over, and we'll watch a movie. I'll make popcorn. Just have a girls night."

"A girls night, okay. But what about some other night?" Troy was starting to wonder what he had gotten himself into. What kind of girl was Ashley? It wasn't that he was against a goody two shoes. He just didn't think they lived life to the fullest. There's nothing quite like a good party.

"I just think that there's more to life than just a party." She removed her napkin to dab her face. She removed some sauce from her corner lip. Troy moved a little uncomfortably in his bench. Ashley noticed; there was that few seconds of awkward silence as both of them tried to decide where to go next in the conversation.

Troy decided to let that line of conversation go for the

moment. “So, how big is your family?” Troy thought that she had a younger brother in elementary, but that's all that he knew.

“I have a younger brother in third grade, Aaron. And I have baby sister who is just 16 months. Her name is Katelyn.”

Troy nodded his head as she spoke wondering what it was like to have siblings. Wondering what it was like to have any kind of normal family.

“Do you have any brothers and sisters?” Ashley didn't think that he did. She had heard some things, like his family was separated. But she didn't know for sure, they didn’t run in the same crowd.

“I don’t have any brothers or sisters. My mom and dad are…” Troy kind of fell silent and looked away a little. Even though he felt the urge to just kind of tell her everything. He was pretty guarded with his emotions. “together.”

Ashley suddenly felt the urge to hold his hand when she saw glimpses of pain flash across Troy’s face, especially when he mentioned his dad. But she kept herself in check. This was their official first date. No matter how cute Troy was, she wasn't just going to come to his rescue. Ashley decided to change the subject.

“So what is your number one movie of all time?” Ashley said.

Troy tried not to break into a smile, "You look very serious. My number one movie of all time?"

Ashley smiled. She titled her head as to say, "continue." Troy couldn't help but notice the green specks in her hazel eyes, as he paused for a minute.

"My number one movie of all time? I think it would probably have to be…" and here he paused deciding whether to tell the truth or to say it was one of those macho movies guys are suppose to like. "Actually, my favorite movie of all time is *The Breakfast Club*."

"*The Breakfast Club*? Isn't that an 80s movie about the teenagers in the library?"

"Yeah, that's the one." Troy had decided to tell the truth about the movie.

"That's interesting. I've actually never seen that movie. It's on like TNT or TBS every once a while. I guess I'll have to see what it's about."

"I don't watch it on television. They edit out all the good parts."

"Maybe we could watch it sometime." Ashley looked up at him through her eyelashes, her hazel eyes stunning his heart. Troy just smiled.

They finished their meal a little after 9:30. Ashley said that she needed to be home by 10. Troy didn’t have a problem with that, but he thought it was a little strict. To pass the little time they had left they decided to walk downtown. Troy liked the way the light shone against the darkness of the sky, creating shields against the darkness.

Troy got Ashley home with five minutes to spare. She got out. He walked her to the front porch. She said goodnight then quickly kissed him on the cheek and without another word entered her house. Surprised, Troy didn't know exactly what to do. His heart felt like it was bursting. He jumped off of the porch steps feeling as if there was nothing wrong in the world.

10 GAME SIX

Troy decided not to go to the party.

His mom was finishing up her hair and lipstick at the door when he walked in. "Oh, hi, honey. Did you have a good time?"

Troy didn't even mind the phony attempt at motherhood. "Yes, I did."

"That's awesome dear. Is she a nice girl?"

"Yes, Mom, she's…." Troy couldn't find the right words, "she's cool."

"That's great." His mom finished her make-up, put a few things into her purse, and kissed him goodbye. He knew that Sunday morning would not be good. He wouldn't see his mom until after lunchtime, but tonight he wasn't going to let that affect him. He headed into the kitchen to find something to snack on. His plan was to play some video games and maybe see who was online.

As Troy was rummaging through the cupboards to find some chips or popcorn, his dad walked in. He could smell the whiskey on his breath. His dad must've started drinking during the college games earlier that day.

"What are you doing home?" His dad asked in a slightly slurred voice.

Troy's good mood was starting to fade. He thought to himself, *how can three people who live in the same house not know what each other was doing?* "I was on a date."

"Oh, so now you're a big shot. Dating because you won three games."

Troy tried to let the memory of the night with Ashley be the filter to his dad's aggression. His dad's sarcasm was the one thing that hit Troy's emotions the fastest. Something in Charlie's tone cut through any defense Troy tried to build. Somehow Charlie could make Troy feel worthless with just a few sarcastic words.

"This was one date."

"So, who is this girl?"

Troy closed his eyes trying to contain his frustration. He

didn't want to discuss this with his dad, especially right now. He knew that his dad was an angry drunk. He may not totally be drunk at the moment, but he could turn angry anyway.

"She's a cheerleader."

"A cheerleader? Your mom used to be a cheerleader. Look where that got us."

Troy couldn't stand all of the comments about how bad life was. Partly because he knew it was true. But also partly because he didn't think his dad did anything to make it better. Troy didn't know what had truly happened between his mom and dad. In fact this was all he could remember of their life. Two separate people still under the same roof. Neither one expressing love for each other but somehow free to do it to other people.

"It's late, I'm going to my room."

"What? Wait a second. I'm not done. I want to know what my son is doing. The big shot running back. For the three and two Vikings."

Troy knew enough that his dad had to vent. If Troy did anything that interrupted him, it would end badly.

"I bet that coach of yours thinks he's got everything figured out. That you'll win the state championship. You guys are nothing." His dad went to the fridge.

Troy stood there for a moment, wondering why his dad hated him, hated Coach Reiner. He promised himself that he wouldn't be like this with his own kids. A flash of life with Ashley crossed his mind. He smiled. A mistake.

"What's so funny?" His dad was in his face before Troy could even blink. Troy was looking into his own eyes, tired, angry, but heavy with years. For a second Troy saw his future but then quickly made a promise to not grow up to be his dad.

"Nothing." Troy backpedaled.

"You think you're going to be something better than your old man? Better than this drunk?" Troy looked at his feet. Usually his dad was angry, but every once and a while he would get depressing, let his ghosts run free.

"I wasn't always a drunk, you know." His dad popped the top of the can and took a long swig. "I had a scholarship."

Troy did know. He knew a few things. He knew his grandfather was also a mean drunk. But Troy never knew why his dad never went to college. It was a mystery that Troy never asked about. Something was different tonight in his dad's voice so Troy kept quiet.

"I was going to play linebacker, for Doane College. I had thought about walking on at Nebraska, but I knew I would get to play at Doane." He paused and took a long swig, finishing the beer. He got up to grab another beer without looking at his son. He continued to talk as he walked back to the table. "I loved football. It was an escape from Grandpa and working in the meat shop."

Troy thought to himself, *well, there's one thing we have in common.*

"Do you know why I didn't go?" His dad looked at him, hard.

"No," Troy said timidly. He was curious and didn't want to do anything to stop his dad from talking. He understood this was a moment when his father was vulnerable. Just maybe he would understand his dad better.

His dad sat there, thinking. His eyes were droopy with alcohol and the weight of the past. The weight of the years sat between them. They were almost strangers. Yet, Troy always wished for more of him. Football wasn't only an escape for Troy but a proving ground. He knew his dad loved football, had heard the stories of his high school days. He remembered sitting at his dad's feet on Saturdays, gladly getting his dad a beer and listening to him coach from the chair. He had thought his dad was the smartest person alive.

Troy would go outside and reenact the game by himself, throwing the ball up in the air and running to catch it. He would change the plays to match what his dad thought the team should have done. Troy's team always won. Funny how Troy thought about that at this moment. Remembering that his dad never joined him, even if Troy asked him to come out and play.

Anger started to press on his chest. Troy wanted to say that he didn't care why his dad didn't go to college. What he wanted to know was why he thought Troy was never good enough.

"Do you know why I didn't play at Doane?"

Troy quietly said no again. Curiosity outweighed his anger.

"You are not an only child," his dad said softly.

Troy didn't register what his dad said. "What?"

In a flash of anger his dad repeated his statement, "You are not my only child. I have another son. You have a half brother." The floodgates of the past opened, and his dad rode the wave after another swallow of beer.

"His name is Rick. He lives with his mother in Missouri. He's a senior at Northwest Missouri State. He runs track." Troy stood there looking at his father, eyes wide, still not grasping that his dad had another life.

"His mother is Sarah Kilnster. She was a cheerleader, too." He stared at his son for a moment, lifting an eyebrow as if to warn him. "She was a senior. We tried to make it work, I swear I tried." His dad turned his eyes from him. Suddenly his face seemed heavy with years, his shoulders dropped, and his hands darkened. "We both had so many dreams we let go of that they built a wall around our hearts. I promised myself that I would not be like my father, like Grandpa."

Troy turned his eyes from his dad at that statement. He felt such a rush of connection to that desire that he felt ashamed to have thought it.

"We didn't last two years. I worked construction, started drinking every night. Things just went bad. I remember holding Rick..." His dad got up, finished his beer and moved to the fridge. His steps were unsteady, but Troy didn't know if it was from the beer or the emotions. "It was the same as when I held you. You both represented a chance for me to make my dreams come true. Not my football dreams, but that idea... that chance to be somebody to someone else. Both of your lives seemed to be in my hands..." His dad paused. "But Sarah was a strong woman. She left me. In the middle of the night, a post-it note on the mirror. A post-it note." He laughed a dark laugh.

"It said 'You are not the man I thought you were. Goodbye.' and she took Rick with her." His dad looked into the past. Troy could see the years playing behind his eyes. "I was not the man she thought I was..."

Troy stood there for a minute. His dad was lost in time, lost in emotions that he never showed. Troy stepped away. The shock of the revelation heavy on his mind. A brother? A half-brother, but a brother. Troy couldn't get his mind around the story. More questions peppered his mind. Did his mom know? When was the last time his dad ever talked to his son? The last question rattled Troy. He closed the door to his room, put his iPhone on shuffle and sat by his window.

"Dr. Stephenson, did you want something?" Coach Reiner knocked on the door of Dr. Stephenson's office.

"Yes, come and sit down."

Dr. Stephenson's office was simple with signs of school pride. He had been the superintendent of the school for six years now. Coach Reiner had learned that he actually taught at Twin Valley fifteen years earlier. And then traveled from job to job a little bit as he continued his schooling. However, he found his way back to Twin Valley.

"That was a heckuva game Friday night. I don't think I've ever seen such a unique defense."

Coach Reiner smiled and said, "From what I saw on tape I thought it would work."

"You know I haven't seen the team play this well in a long time. I think you're doing a solid job."

"Thanks, Dr. Stephenson. But really, the boys decided that they wanted something better. They deserve most of the credit. They finally, I think, bought into what we're trying to do."

"Well, you gave them something to believe in. I was just looking through some old records. I don't think our offense has gained that much yardage on the ground before, or our defense given up so much yardage in the air before."

Coach Reiner didn't quite know how to take that last comment. "Well, we had to bend, but I am glad we didn't break."

"Yes, I didn't mean anything by it, Coach. Just saying, what a crazy game it was. So how do you think we'll do against St. Michael's?"

"Are you asking do you think we can win? Honestly, I don't know. St. Michael's is a powerhouse. Do you want to know if I think we will play well? Yes, but I think this may be more of a mental hurdle then a physical one."

Dr. Stephenson sat back in this chair, "What do you mean?"

Coach Reiner took a second to think. "I mean I don't know if the boys totally believe in their talents. They know that they can play, and we've played good ball this year except in our second game. But a team like St. Michaels, with their tradition, is more of a mental challenge for them to overcome. This game will not be a test of how well they play football, it will be a test of how much they believe in themselves and what they can do."

Dr. Stephenson sat up and nodded. "You're right. St.

Michael's has been in the playoffs every year I can remember. They have won the state title four times in the last ten years, I believe. But from what I see, I think we have a good chance."

"Well, we will need a little bit of help from the football gods. We will need some breaks go our way in a game like this. But I think they are ready to play. I think if we set the tone right away, stay focused, then we'll see what happens."

Both of the men turned as they heard sirens go through town. They looked at each other wondering what the emergency was. Dr. Stevenson said, "I just wanted to chat with you for a few and see how things are going."

"Thanks, Dr. Stephenson. You know, overall, it's been a pretty good year. I'm excited for the upcoming game."

"Ok, guys, over here."

Amazing what a three-game winning streak will do for a team.

"Now, this is our test week. We have St. Michael's on Saturday. That means we get off schedule. That means our focus gets challenged. That means we face a football team that has been in the play-offs for the last five years. That means we meet them on their home turf."

The team settled down. Reality has a way of bringing focus back.

"Today is Tuesday. I decided we will get off schedule today." The team looked at each other with questions. "Friday will be our pregame practice, Thursday our defense and offense game plan practice, and Wednesday will be our conditioning and learning practice."

A hand shot up from the crowd. Teon had a question, "So, what is today?"

"How did I know you would ask?" The team laughed. "Well, we are going to warm-up like we always do, then it is opposite flag football." Teon's hand shot up again.

"Give me a second, Teon." Coach Reiner smiled at Teon. He returned the smile. "Players will play the opposite of their normal positions."

That got them rallied up again. Some of the linemen were already talking smack.

"I'll show you how a big man runs."

"Wait till you see my arm."

"Call me train, because you won't stop me."

Coach Reiner blew his whistle. "OK, OK, let's get started with warm-ups." The boys found their way into lines still chatting about how awesome they were going to be in the flag football game.

Coach Reiner walked among them as they moved through the routine. Coach Reiner was chatting with Kyle when he noticed the three men approaching the practice field. He made out Mr. Henderson, the principal, and Dr. Stephenson. As the men came closer he could tell that the third person was a policeman. Coach Reiner's gut turned. He noticed the way they walked, as if they really didn't want to cross this line but knew they had to. Coach Reiner walked to meet them.

"Coach.... Something has happened." Mr. Henderson said. His eyes darted to the team, back to Coach Reiner, back to the team, then back again to Coach. "Jason's dad..." and Mr. Henderson's voice broke. The policeman stepped forward.

"Mr. Petersen suffered a heart attack sometime this morning. But no one knew. He died in the fields. Mrs. Petersen discovered him around two when he hadn't come in for lunch. The family is gathering at the hospital."

Coach Reiner turned his head to see if the team had heard any of it. He doubted they did, they were standing a ways away, but the team knew something was going on. They had stopped stretching and were watching the interaction between their coach and the three men.

“I've come to take Jason to the hospital. Do you want to come along?” The policeman asked.

Coach Reiner thought for a moment. What was the best choice here? He would need to handle the team. Jason would have his family. “No, I'll stay here... to break it to the team.”

Coach Reiner turned, and tried to sound casual as he called Jason over. The team went silent. They knew Jason could not be in trouble. That meant something else had happened to involve a policeman.

Coach Reiner let the cop start the story; he put his hand on Jason's shoulder. As the officer explained that his dad had died, Jason went blank. His eyes deepened in their focus, as if he suddenly could see the field, see his dad lying there trying to climb into the tractor to reach his phone. Jason saw his dad turn from the door and face him.

The officer brought Jason back with a question he had

already asked, "You ready to go?"

Coach Reiner headed back to the team as Jason, surrounded by the three men, headed to the hospital. Coach Reiner was quickly running through his head how to handle this moment.

"Coach, what's wrong?"

"Yeah, what's going on?"

"Did Jason do something?"

"OK, guys... listen." Coach Reiner couldn't get the words to connect. There were no books or workshops on how to handle situations like this. The simple truth found its way out. "Jason's dad died from a heart attack while he was out in the field."

Silence. Each boy suddenly faced with a reality about his own father. That no matter how much you love them or hate them, there will come a day when a son says goodbye to his father, just not at this age. Coach Reiner allowed the silence to linger, to allow them to process their own thoughts. He watched as the boys began to turn their thoughts to Jason and his dad, their faces opening up to express disbelief. Jason and his dad were a staple in the community. Mr. Petersen was at every activity his kids were in. During the summer Jason and his dad were always seen together, working, or fishing from the back of their truck.

Coach Reiner unconsciously rubbed the bridge of his nose. "All right, guys. This is..." He took a breath. "Right now the game of football takes a back seat, and our football team, especially Jason, takes precedence. Don't take this the wrong way, but do not bombard him right now. Yes, send him a text or call. But understand that his family is..." Coach Reiner's mind stumbled. The team had all eyes on him. They were looking to him for answers, for directions. "They have to have time, at this moment,"

Coach Reiner just let his heart speak. "They are trying to understand this, just like you. The pain will come fast. Jason will need every one of us over the next couple of days. But also, we will need each other. If you need anything, call one of us." Coach Reiner motioned to Coach Sanders and Coach Keller.

Coach Sanders nodded, "Call anytime. Anytime."

Coach Keller nodded also, but had that far off look. Coach Reiner placed his hand on his back and said, "This is our team, and we do this together."

They sat on the open tailgate of Jason's truck. It was 9:30 in the evening. The stars were in full force, sprinkling the sky like glitter.

Teon didn't know what to say. He had not lost anyone in his family before. Of course, he thought all he really had was his mom. No matter how hard he tried, he couldn't see life without her. Her forced optimism in the morning. Teon knew she was tired. That she was lonely. But she always had breakfast for him and a kiss as he headed out the door.

A snippet of a rap song shattered the quietness. Teon reached for his phone. It was his mom wanting to know how Jason was doing. Teon quickly typed a reply, turned off the ringer, and placed the phone back in his pocket. He ignored the phone as it vibrated a few seconds later. He knew it was his mom saying something about being safe.

"My mom wanted to know how you were doing…" Teon said. After a few awkward seconds he followed up with, "She's still at work."

Jason just sat there. Watching the small silver reflections of the river flow by. The moon was just past half full, so it provided some light to the riverbank. Jason had been asked that question for the last two days. Tomorrow it would be the first thing everyone asked him. He didn't know the answer.

The night didn't provide one.

Teon decided not to push the topic, but the stillness of the situation was making him antsy. The whole situation seemed surreal. Most of life seemed normal. Tomorrow morning would be the same routine, school would be normal, and then practice. Yet, nothing would be normal tomorrow for Jason. Teon knew this, but couldn't actually make it make sense. He turned to look at Jason. Did Jason have these same thoughts?

As if he read his mind Jason muttered, “How am I doing?”

Then the darkness of the night settled back in between them for a few minutes.

“I'm tired of hearing that, and tomorrow... That's all anyone will ask. Do you know what people used to ask me about?” Jason didn't wait for Teon to answer. Teon didn't try.

“My dad... They would ask, 'How's your Dad?' I used to hate answering that question, not because of my dad.” Emotion edged his voice. “But because most of the people didn't really care. They were just making small talk. They could have headed to Sandy's in the morning to talk to him. Him and the boys...”

Teon remembered how during the summer Mr. Petersen would take a break around eight most mornings. Mr. Petersen would pause; check his beat up Timex and say, "Time for me to check in with the boys." That meant it was time for a break. He and Jason would head to the house, while Mr. Petersen got in his truck and headed to town.

"They aren't going to ask that anymore." Jason said.

Teon didn't understand, "Huh?"

"Ask how my dad..."

Somehow the darkness gained weight. It sat heavy on their shoulders. Jason was thinking how tomorrow would be different, but he didn't didn't know what to do about it. Both of the boys seemed to understand a glancing secret of life. The routine of daily life was just a facade to cover the uncertainty of what will happen next. The routine gave people strength to make the next decision, to move forward, to accomplish things. It kept the reality that we have no control of the next hidden moment. If we saw how random actions could change everything, we wouldn't be able to make a decision, to move, to live. The cover of routine was such a strong facade that when life's chaos breaks through we are left powerless, unable to move. Yet, routine quickly recovers, and life moves in a predictable manner again. Leaving two young men sitting on the tailgate of a truck confused and scared.

The team sat quietly in the auditorium. They knew why they were here. Forty-eight hours ago the world tilted with the loss of Mr. Petersen. But the sun rose, and the school bell rang. Many of the players were awed by how life seemed to continue around them while inside they couldn't come to grips with how to handle this situation.

Coach Reiner walked downed the aisle. It was his call to make, but this was a team issue. “I know you know why we are here. The funeral will be Friday. I don't think Jason will play.” He paused, “Honestly, I'm not sure how we will play. The decision we have is simple. We play the game, or we forfeit.”

Coach Reiner let the statement sit in the air. He made himself wait.

“We can't reschedule the game?” Troy asked.

“No, we can't. Let me be honest, it is okay not to play this game. We are in the middle of one of those big moments in life. This is a challenge that all of us will face ourselves sometime in our life, but right now one of our teammates is in the middle of it." Coach Reiner said.

"Coach," Kyle started to ask, "Is it okay to play?"

Coach Reiner paused to consider the best answer. "Yes, it is also okay to play. Mr. Petersen was one of our biggest fans. I think he would be honored if we played." Coach Reiner stopped. The team turned to see Jason and his mom walking toward them.

"Coach, is it OK if I play?" Jason asked.

Coach Reiner looked to Mrs. Petersen. She smiled softly and nodded to answer the question in Coach Reiner's expression.

Teon got up from his seat. He and Jason slapped hands and hugged with the other arm. "This is your team, bro."

Jason replied, "No, this is *our* team."

Coach Reiner had to fight back tears. For all the headaches teenagers caused him, they also had the power to change everything with their honesty. "Is it all right if we play the game, Coach?" Jason asked again.

"Yes, yes it is." The team cheered unexpectedly. Coach Reiner let them express their emotions for a minute. "OK, well, it is just after four, we better get to practice."

A sarcastic "Ahhh" came from the team, but there were smiles as they left the auditorium.

Coach Reiner walked with Mrs. Petersen. "I know you are probably tired of hearing it, but how are you doing? Is there anything I can do for you?"

Mrs. Petersen smiled tiredly at him, "My husband said you were a good man; he was honored to have you coach Jason."

Coach Reiner smiled back, uncomfortable with the praise at such a moment as this.

"But, Jason hasn't shown much emotion, Coach. I think he needs football to channel his emotions. Would you keep an extra eye on him?" She stopped at the door. "I don't want Jason to just man up through this. He and his dad were quiet people, but his dad knew how to let his feelings out, both bad and good." She was now twisting her wedding ring. "I fear Jason doesn't know how to let this pain out. You know what I mean?"

Coach Reiner nodded.

Mrs. Petersen stared at her ring, losing herself in memories of a good life that now was altered. "I think football can help, just please, keep an eye on him." She looked up at Coach Reiner, tears welling in her eyes.

"I will," Coach Reiner said. She silently walked down the hall. Coach Reiner couldn't help asking himself why bad things happen to good people as he headed out to the practice field.

The church was an old cathedral type church. The celling seemed to rise to the heavens. The walls of the church had beautiful stained glassed windows that depicted different religious scenes. There were two sets of wooden pews that ran the length of the church. Every pew was filled. Coach Reiner was sitting with most of the football team. A few of the freshmen were sitting with their parents.

There was to be a reception at the City Hall after the graveyard service. It was about 15 minutes before the service was to begin; Coach Reiner could hear the soft sobbing of different family members. He was amazed at how many people were actually at the church, but it didn't surprise him. Dan Petersen was a good man.

Coach Reiner found Mrs. Petersen and simply shook her hand. He mumbled that he was sorry. Sometimes life's biggest moments left you stumbling for words. She took his hand and gave him a hug. Coach Reiner could only hold back the tears as he grabbed his wife's hand and sat down a few pews from the front.

Teon was the only football player besides Jason to be a pallbearer. The rest of the pallbearers were family. Dan had three brothers and one sister. Coach Reiner didn't recognize all the pallbearers. The Petersen family had so many cousins and other family members that lived in the area.

The church was filled with bouquets of flowers, most of them reflecting the school colors. The high cathedral ceiling echoed with the music.

Jason was the only person to speak at the funeral besides the priest. As he stood before the crowd, you could see that he was working at staying composed. He spoke slowly but steadily. Mrs. Petersen could be heard weeping as her son spoke.

"I first want to say thank you to everyone who came here today to honor my dad. I want to thank friends and family and people that just knew my dad. My dad was my greatest hero. He taught me the meaning of hard work. He taught me the meaning of family, and he taught me why it was important to live up to your word."

Jason took a pause. He was not close to tears, but he was gaining confidence just speaking about his dad.

"He taught me the what it means to be a man. To be strong. To be a man that others can count on. Just like I could count on him. I don't know why this happened. And I'll be honest; I may not want to know. But I am thankful for the seventeen years that he was my dad. And I know that he will be my dad every day of my life."

Coach Reiner didn't think that there was a dry eye in the place. Even the old men's club in the back were dabbing their face with the red handkerchiefs they carried.

"Again, I want to thank everyone for coming. It amazes me how much my dad meant to all of you. My mom, and I, and my sister say thank you and God bless."

There weren't as many people at the graveyard service. The family asked only a few people to come. Coach Reiner and all the senior football players were there.

After the casket was lowered into the ground, most of the family headed to the reception. Coach Reiner stayed for a few minutes standing next to Jason.

Julie had gone to the car. She told him to take as much time as he needed. "You don't have to play tomorrow, Jason. They won't know, but it's not that important."

"Honestly, Coach I don't much feel like playing football. But I think my dad would want me to. And I think it would actually do me good."

"If you don't make it to walk-through practice this evening we're loading the bus at 11 o'clock tomorrow."

"Yeah, is all right if I don't go to practice tonight?"

"Yes, it is. But you're more than welcome to come to practice." Coach Reiner placed his hand on his shoulder. "Your dad was a good man. And I think the greatest example of that is you."

Jason visually held back his emotions. "I'll see you tomorrow, Coach."

Coach Reiner stopped at the reception for a little while. The mood had started to shift. You could hear laughter as stories started to flow. Coach Reiner and his wife shared a piece of cake listening to the stories. It was still 2 1/2 hours before walk-through practice. He conversed with some of the community members and watched a slideshow of Dan's life. The photos ranged from fun elementary pictures, to high school football pictures, to family and farm life pictures. Jason's dad wasn't always smiling, but his eyes held a steady joy that couldn't be denied. Especially the pictures with his children and wife.

Coach Reiner again gave Jason's mom and his little sister a hug. Jason appeared just as Coach Reiner was leaving. Coach Reiner needed to get to practice; he motioned to some of the football players that it was time to go. They said they would be there soon.

Coach Reiner sat with a cup of coffee on the couch. Julie sat next to him. Not sure how to answer the last question. Her husband had asked if he had done the right thing. Meaning to go ahead go ahead and okay playing the game against St. Michael's. Even with Jason wanting to play.

"I know that football is not the most important thing at the moment. Does this make it more important?"

"I think I would play. I mean there are many moments like when Brett Favre played. But that was the pros." Coach Reiner looked at his wife. He trusted her insight more than anyone else.

"I don't know, hon. I wish I had an answer to this. "Julie wrapped her arms around his arm and set her head on his shoulder.

"I know that football is important to these boys, and to you, and to the community. Is playing the game right or wrong? I don't think there is an answer to that."

David sipped his coffee and knew that she was right in that there was not a right or wrong answer. They had decided as a team to play the game. And if he believed what he was trying to instill in the team then he would have to go with the team's decision. Coach Reiner had asked Coach Keller and Coach Sanders their thoughts. Both of them stated that it was his decision to make, however, they both hinted that playing the game might be important enough for the whole community.

David took another sip of his coffee. His next thought was how was he going to handle getting the team ready to play. He wondered what, if any, type of inspirational message he could give them. Anything he thought of paled against the reality of what that their teammate, Jason, was going through. His job was to get them ready. He kissed his wife on the forehead.

"Hon, I know that no matter what, you tried to do your best. Sometimes that has to be enough," Julie said.

"That's why I married you, beautiful." David sipped his

coffee then asked his wife. "What should we do for dinner?"

Coach Reiner was worried. The bus was awfully quiet for the 45-minute drive to the game. The reality of the funeral yesterday felt heavy in the bus. No one knew exactly what to say to Jason. When everyone loaded onto the bus, there was normal interaction, but as the bus ride continued it became silent.

That worried him.

Jason didn't seem any different on the surface. He was always relatively quiet on bus rides. The only time he spoke was to keep the underclassmen under control. But today Jason didn't say anything to anybody. He only seemed to stare at the passing landscape out the window.

Coach Reiner knew that this was the game to measure how good they actually were. St. Michael's was a powerhouse. They had been in the playoffs for twelve straight years, winning four state titles. They had a winning tradition that Coach Reiner wanted for the Vikings.

Coach Reiner knew that the team was better but he didn't know if they were good enough or could focus today to pull off an upset. If anything, life had taught him that you still had to play the game. Anything was possible on any football field. But with the loss of Jason's dad, that created a hurdle they might not be able to overcome.

As the team took the field for special teams warm-up, Coach Reiner was in a better mood. The locker room speeches seemed to get the team focused on football, if only for the afternoon. All the Coaches shook their heads as the speakers began playing soft rock music. The Knights were not on the field yet. Coach Reiner knew that it was a small psychological trick to get the energy level down. So he tried to be louder than the music as he barked instructions for the punters and field-goal kickers.

To his surprise, the soft rock music actually lifted their spirits as players started to mockingly sing love songs to each other as they fielded punts. He didn't mind a little bit of goofing off to relieve the stress that they dealt with yesterday. Even Jason was smiling every once a while as he got his ankles taped on the sideline. Sam was singing into the water bottles.

Coach Reiner shook his head a little bit as the Saint Michael's Knights came out onto the field, and the music started to play

AC/DC. *Interesting song choice,* he thought. With the energy building in the stadium, the St. Michael's team seemed to outnumber the Vikings three to one. The Knights seem to take up their whole side of the field during team warm-ups. The Vikings looked like a junior high team in numbers. But Coach Reiner felt confident. The warm-ups seem to be taking on a serious note. Jason led the team with more bite to his commands.

Things started out well for the Vikings; they won the toss and chose to take the ball. They were going to try to score first. They didn't, but they gained 42 yards before they had to punt. The drive stalled outside of field-goal range.

The Vikings held the Knights to only six plays on their first possession of the game. But then things slowly started to turn.

In the second quarter Troy fumbled trying to reach out for a first down. St. Michael's recovered. The Knights scored two plays later on a counter trap.

The Vikings had a great kick return brought back because of a holding call. They went three and out. The Knights returned the punt for a touchdown. 14 to 0 in just minutes. Coach Reiner felt his team fall into quicksand. Nothing they did seemed to work. The harder they tried, the worse the outcome. At half time the Knights were up 21 to 3. The Vikings scored on a long field goal to end the first half.

Coach Reiner didn't know what to say. He didn't know if he should yell, or console, or actually even how to handle the situation. How do you tell a team that it matters to play football the day after one of their teammate's fathers passed away? How do you let them know that it's important to overcome adversity even in the smallest things, to handle moments like Jason was going through? Especially when he knew nobody would fault them for losing. But just because you have an excuse to lose doesn't mean that it's still okay to lose.

The locker room was filled with negative energy. Teammates were quiet but snipping at each other about failed assignments. Jason sat quietly in the corner getting new tape around his ankle.

Coach Reiner stepped forward to speak but couldn't find the words. He asked Coach Keller to cover the defense and the reads that they would need to change. Coach Sanders also discussed the receivers' routes and the coverage the Knights were playing. The team then waited silently for Coach Reiner's words. He just didn't know what to do. so he was honest with them. "I wish I could make this some inspirational moment. Some inspirational quote or speech. This is just a game. Yesterday we dealt with life."

Jason turned his head at the mention of his dad's funeral, but he remained quiet.

"I don't have any ideas right now. I've never had to deal with anything like this before. I wish I could tell you that everything will be fine. That you'll never have another heartbreaking moment. That you will never feel crippled and beaten to the floor."

Coach Reiner kneeled down in the middle of the locker room, "I know that this loss can be excused. That our fans will not think anything differently of us if St. Michael's wins this game, but a habit of losing is not what we're about."

"Habits are formed at the hardest moments in our lives. Jason is still a son. Jason is still a teammate. And Jason will someday probably be a father. Life has house rules, and it is our reaction to those house rules that build our lives."

Coach Reiner slowed down to catch his thoughts, "I know that we will probably not win this game, but it does not mean that you do not try. To give your best at any moment in life is what we're called to do. As men, as fathers, as sons, and as friends. That is our role. That is what we do. So let's go out there and work on what we need to work on. We will let the game handle itself. Because every moment in life, positive or negative, calls on you to be your best."

Jason stood up, tears forming in his eyes, but his voice was steady, "We will do our best, and I know we may lose, but you know what? We will do this together."

The team followed Jason out to do halftime warm-ups. Coach Reiner looked exhausted. Coach Keller patted him on the shoulder.

The Vikings played well in the second half. They scored two touchdowns. The defense kept the Knights to 10 points. 31 to 17, it was a moral victory, if there was such a thing. The bus ride home was loud, with laughter. Coach Reiner was okay with that.

11 GAME SEVEN

The rain was a now a curtain. Coach Reiner couldn't see the visitor's sideline. The refs said they would call the game if there was lightning, but would play through the rain. Coach Reiner's play sheet was in pieces on the ground, it had disintegrated from the rain.

"Time out!" Coach Reiner signaled as he approached the side judge. "Time out!" The whistle blew.

The Vikings were down by four with three minutes left in the third quarter. It was hard to run the ball. It was impossible to throw. The middle of the field was mud. The team huddled in close to hear him.

"We need to get out of the middle of the field. Indy Left, Zip, 28 Swing."

"Coach, can we do this out of shotgun? I can't get my feet set in the mud." Mike said.

"Kyle? Can you get it back to him?" Coach Reiner asked his center.

"Yes, Coach." Kyle never said more than what was needed.

Coach Reiner patted him on the top of his helmet. "I thought so. Okay, Houston Left, Zip, 28 swing."

For a moment Coach Reiner thought about the crowed. He wondered what they could see. How many were in the stands? Coach Reiner was happy that his wife had decided to stay home. He turned his mind back to the game as the team broke the huddle. They were on their own 45-yard line. It was second and eight.

The line judge stood with the ball under his coat. The crew was switching the balls every two downs. Kevin, the ball boy, had given up trying to keep the balls dry. He now set his efforts on getting the mud off.

"Ready?" The line judge asked as Kyle stepped up to the line.

"Yes, sir." Kyle replied as he set his feet.

The line judge set the ball down with the laces up. The teams set their lines. There was no jumping around, linebackers set their bodies to face their gaps, DBs got into a wider athletic position. The receivers set like stone. No one was going to risk losing their footing.

Mike surveyed the defense as a habit. The weather had canceled any adjustments. "Blue 78..." Mike paused. 1, 2, 3, ... 11? As Mike scanned the second time his quarterback instincts kicked in. They had all eleven players in. The safeties were sitting about eight yards back. Even with the shotgun formation they were playing all out run. Black 30 series flashed across his mind.

Teon would still come across in motion. Jay would still swing. But instead of blocking the backer, Teon would release for a flag route, Cam would block and release. Could he make that pass? Coach Reiner's voice piped up in his head, "You are the leader on the field. Lead." Mike wanted this game for Jason, for this team to get back above .500. Nothing would be lost if he simply ran the play. Coach Reiner had called it. Coach was taking the chance on a pass play; the audible wouldn't be any different.

"Black 34. Black 34." Mike called out. Teon crossed his face. Mike swore he saw a smile. "Set.... Hut!"

Teon was a yard left of Cam. He turned slowly, both playing the look of a blocking route and getting his feet set to head up field. Teon recognized what Mike saw. The safeties were too close to the line of scrimmage. Even now they were stepping toward the line of scrimmage, keying in on Troy's swing pattern. Cameron sat on his route instead of engaging the corner. Teon headed up field, lifting his feet up and out of the mud. Teon and the free safety, number 12, locked eyes. The safety made the assumption Teon was headed to block him and headed inside of Teon to try to miss the block to pursue Troy. Teon took his seventh step and then with his left foot pushed off at an angle toward the sideline.

Coach Reiner had heard the audible, and held his breath. He knew it was the right call, but the rain… But everything. Jason had not said a word all game long. He was having a solid game, trying to find some normalness in football. Winning this game would get them back above .500 and a real chance at the play-offs. Coach Reiner let his breath out as Teon broke for the sideline.

Kyle snapped the ball well, considering. Mike turned the ball in his hands. Laces finding their place between his fingers. The weeks of practice started the clock in his head. One, set his feet. Two, check for pressure, none. Three, don't release yet... Mike knew the route would not be in the same rhythm. He waited a heartbeat more than the timer in his head.

Coach Reiner could see the ball release from Mike's hand. His first thought was that Mike had gripped the ball too tight. The football wobbled, but the rotation kept it from becoming a duck. Coach Reiner turned his eyes to Teon's route. Teon was gaining speed as he moved onto the part of the field with grass. Teon needed to catch up with the ball though. Mike had put some force behind his throw. Coach Reiner leaned onto the field. Both Teon and the ball were fading into the rain. The side judge was already moving down field. Coach Reiner waited for the whistle to blow.

The sideline was silent. Just the stream of rain. Coach Reiner couldn't believe he wasn't hearing a whistle. Then from somewhere he heard the announcer yell, "Touchdown! No way! We scored." A whistle blew to confirm the statement. The sideline exploded.

"Two. Going for two. Nice throw, Mike." Mike had run to the sideline to get the call.

"Thanks, Coach. What's the call?" Mike was trying to keep his excitement under control; there was still another quarter to play.

"Indy 33. Tell Jason we need a path."

"Right, Coach."

Mike headed to the 12-yard line where the team was waiting.

A surge of pride swept through him. The team was huddled and ready. They knew this game wasn't over. The defense was rumbling on the other side of the ball. Mike recognized the behavior, which was them last year, at times. More concerned with whom to blame than the next play.

"Nice catch, Teon." The team responded in agreement. For once Teon only smiled and raised his hand as if to say thank you, but let's play.

"Ok, Indy 33 dive. Jason we need a path. Coach's orders." For the first time everyone actually looked at him. Jason nodded. Mike couldn't tell if it was rain or tears on Jason's cheeks.

The team lined up in the I formation, snapped the ball, and Troy followed Jason in for the two-point conversion.

"Kick-off team, on me." Coach Sanders gathered the kickoff team together. Coach Sanders reminded them to keep their strides short and choppy. "Let's get this game boys."

As the team headed onto the field Coach Reiner turned to see Jason standing before him. "We'll win this game, Coach." Jason said.

"Yes, I believe we will, but we still have a quarter to play." Coach Reiner said.

Without a pause Jason said, “My dad won't let us lose this game. I can feel him smiling, Coach.” The tears were now clear. “I think he is... I know he's proud.”

Coach Reiner didn't know what to say. Sometimes life is just too raw to respond. “I know he is, Jason.” Coach Reiner tapped Jason's shoulder pads. “Let's finish this game.”

The locker room smelled of mud and grass. A blanket of musky aroma hit the coaches as they entered the ruckus. The rain was finally abating. The Vikings had won 14 to 10. The fourth quarter was a stalemate. Neither team could move or handle the ball well. The team had kept its cool and played through the bad breaks the weather had caused.

“All right, settle down. Settle down.” Coach Keller's voice carried through the noise. The boys found a place to sit or stand. “That was a hard fought victory, men. That is some old school football.” Coach Keller took an exaggerated sniff. “I love the smell of grass, mud, and victory.”

The team exploded again. High-fiving each other. Stories breaking out between players. Coach Reiner stood in the doorway, not needing to say anything. Sometimes coaches can talk too much. Coach Keller and Coach Sanders started to discuss the rain. Mike raised his fist in the air, "Hey. Hey. HEY!"

The team settled back down.

"We have been here before, guys. This is our fourth win. Same as last year. But we have two more games. Two more games to win and we will be in the play-offs!" The team exploded again.

"Hey, hey, hey... guys!" Mike hollered.

The team took a few minutes to settle down. Mike let a pause hang in the air. Coach Reiner stepped into the middle of the room, not sure what was going on. Mike choked back the emotion, "This victory is for you, Jason. We are team."

Jason had been enjoying the moment, but now turned to face Mike without a word.

For a long moment the locker room became a picture, a moment in time that burned its colors on their hearts. Teon broke the silence, "Team, Jason." Then he broke the picture by hugging Jason. In an unscripted move the whole team surrounded them, each player murmuring "team" as they joined the huddle.

Coach Reiner turned and motioned to his assistants. In

unison the coaches exclaimed, "team" as they completed the circle.

Jason finished showering, got dressed, and headed out of the locker room. The storm had passed, and the night smelled musky with the rain. Jason felt clean of grief, if for only a little while.

The night was dark. Jason wondered what to do next. He knew a lot of people were gathering at The Bend, but he just didn't feel like messing with that tonight.

He got into his truck and turned up the radio a little bit. He started to drive. As he drove through the town he decided he didn't want all the lights and headed off to the back roads. His mind wouldn't stay off the topic of his dad. He wondered what he would do next year. Who would handle the farm? His plan was to go to college to study agricultural business. But now he wondered what would happen to his future. Could an uncle take over the ranch until he returned? His long-term plan was always to come back home to work with his dad. Jason enjoyed the outdoors and the work involved in running a farm. He had dreams of starting his own family and just living life, a lot like his dad did.

Jason drove onto some gravel road. His truck was able to

handle the wet gravel. He wasn't worried about that. But everything looked foreign to him at the moment. He started to feel panicky as he tried to recognize some landmarks.

That rush of being lost eclipsed his thoughts for the moment. He couldn't see any lights except for the small dots of farm lights. He didn't recognize any trees or fields. The whole world seemed different to him.

As he continued to drive he came upon a country metal bridge. Jason recognized it. It was the bridge that ran over the county line. He had been driving longer than he thought.

He parked his truck next to the bridge out of the way of traffic. Even though he doubted if any traffic would be there this evening. The clouds were starting to clear. He could see stars in the gaps of the clouds. Jason found an old log to sit on. He picked up some pebbles to throw into the small creek.

He started to talk with God. He presented all his questions as he threw each stone into the water. The only response was the babbling of the creek and the crickets and bullfrogs. But that seemed to be a good answer to Jason.

The Bend was crowded after the win. There was a crowd of kids around a car. Mike gathered with a lot of the other kids to help Amber get her car unstuck. His wondered where Jason was. Jason's truck would be able to get Amber's car out of the mud. At first everybody was kind of hesitant to actually get their hands dirty. But as the situation just got messier, everybody got lost in the moment of pulling and pushing and getting splattered from the tires.

Mike got in the front of the car, and he pushed with all his might. That's it when his footing slipped, before he knew it he was under the car. Kyle hollered, "Stop! Stop!"

For a second no one could actually find Mike. It was as if he had disappeared into the ground. But then suddenly Mike's hands appeared on the grill. He pulled himself out from underneath the car. Luckily, it looked like he had a road rash down his shin but it was still pretty painful.

"Holy shit! Mike what was that?"

Mike was shaken. He spit mud and stones out of his mouth. Then asked somebody for a drink.

"I'll get you something. Man, that was crazy!"

Mike shivered as he thought of how fast everything had

happened. He looked down at his rest of his body again; checking to make sure everything was all right. His leg smarted. He could feel the blood and mud mixing but he thought he would be ok.

"I better head for home," Mike said.

Most of the football players around him shook their head in agreement. The night was getting a little out of hand. When the football players left, most of the other students followed suit. Amber's car would have to wait. She would get it out the next day.

The house was silent, as usual. Mike opened the first aid kit from the kitchen. There was another one just like it in both of the bathrooms. Mike put a towel under his leg. He rubbed his leg with a wet cloth, feeling small pebbles lodge free from his skin. He then dabbed a cotton ball with hydrogen peroxide and applied it to the cuts. Mike grimaced as the wounds fizzed. The pain actually felt good. It made the silence of the house disappear. Somehow the pain made him feel more alive. As the hydrogen peroxide settled down, the quiet of the house returned. Mike sat for a few seconds listening to the silence. His heart swelled with loneliness.

Mike rubbed his wound till it started to bleed again. He added hydrogen peroxide again to the wound; the pain eliminated the silence of the house.

David knew that it was a little late, but he felt the need to talk to his own dad. “Hello? Hi, Mom. Did I wake you? Sorry.”

“No, dear. I was just watching Home Shopping Network. You know I enjoy just watching them try to sell the merchandise.” His mom chuckled.

“Is Dad awake?”

“I think he might've fallen asleep in the La-Z-Boy downstairs. Let me go get him.”

“Hello, Son.” His dad didn't sound sleepy. He probably had been watching the news. His parents lived in Colorado. They had moved there a couple of years ago. They decided to get a smaller house and move closer to the rivers and parks. His dad loved fly-fishing. It was not an activity that he and his dad shared.

As the little boy, David remembered trying to fly-fish and just never really got the hang of it. But he would sit and watch his dad fluidly flick the rod. Sitting on the bank, trying to see when the fly would hit the water.

“Hi, Dad.”

"How did the game go tonight?"

"Good. We are now four and three with two games left."

"Four wins already. That's better than last year, correct?"

"Yeah, we have a real shot to make the playoffs this year if we win both games. With the way the wildcard system is set up, we should get in if we win just one of the games. Being above .500 gets us in the playoffs in our class."

"That's good. How is the team playing? How is that kid, I forgot his name."

"Jason."

"Yeah, that's right, Jason. How is he doing?"

"He had a good game tonight. I think that, you know, he is adjusting to life. "

"I bet. How are you doing?"

"I don't know, Dad. I didn't think it would be this hard. Not hard, but like I don't know." It was amazing how much he felt like a teenager talking to his dad. Still intimidated by the fact that he was in the presence of his father. "I mean, I know football is just a game, but it's what I love. I love what it teaches. But there is so much more that happens outside of football. It just seems like everybody's got a hurdle they have to overcome."

His dad said, "Well, Son, everybody does have a hurdle. Sometimes they are small things we can easily overcome. Other times the hurdle is more like a wall. But that's your job. Through football to equip them to be able to handle any hurdle they face."

"I know that, but I guess sometimes I wish that all we had to really worry about was the game plan for the next opponent. Not deal with all this stuff outside of football." David was rubbing the bridge of his nose while thinking about all the extra responsibilities that came with the job.

"But that's exactly what life is, Son. It's a combination of everything you do. You're just getting a taste of what it's like to be involved in the foundation of someone else's life."

"Yeah, I just didn't know." David gathered his thoughts; "I guess I was just kind of naïve that life is hard for some people, unnecessarily hard. "

"Well, you will know that even more when you're a father. When you are have the sole responsibility of another person in the family." His dad just started to laugh. "Wait till your first doctor's appointment for your child, or the first time they are sick. As a dad, or the coach, in your situation, you have to take on the responsibility to take care of them."

"I don't think I'm going to having any young ones running around anytime soon."

"Don't tell your mom that. She's waiting to be a grandma. She's saving up all her nickels to spoil her grandchildren."

"Yeah, I can imagine."

"I think you're doing all right, Son. Just remember that football is a game. It is a powerful game. Use it to build something for somebody's kids. "

"I know. I'm trying to. It's just been a rough couple of weeks."

"There's nothing wrong with rough spots in life. It's how you handle them that makes a difference."

"Thanks, Dad, tell mom we love her. Good night "

"Good night. Good luck next week."

"Thanks, good night." David hung up the phone and headed off to bed. He was planning on getting up early to start game planning for the Bearcats.

Troy and Ashley were sitting on a park bench. They hadn't said much the last couple of minutes, but it felt okay. Her hand was nestled in his. Her fingers were smooth and slender, and they seemed to fit like a glove.

Troy wondered if one person could make life that much better. He wanted to say something but somehow the evening asked for silence. Ashley was the one who actually broke it.

"I hate to ruin the night, but I do have to be home in 30 minutes." Troy understood and didn't want to make anything bad for Ashley from her parents.

Ashley's dad was one of the vice presidents of the local bank. Her mom was active in the PTO and was always doing things to help with school spirit. He didn't want this moment to end.

"Okay. We'll start heading back in a few minutes."

"So, what are you thinking about? "Ashley asked.

"Nothing really, just enjoying sitting here with you. Kind of tired. That was a crazy game. I don't think I've ever ran through so much mud before."

"Yeah, I was a soggy mess within five minutes," Ashley said, laughing, while she scooted in just a little closer. "But that was an intense game. I couldn't even see half of the football team or even the stands."

Troy laughed, imagining what she had looked like with her hair sopping wet and sticking to her head. During the game he couldn't even see the cheerleaders. Not that he was actually looking. The weather had focused them as a team. You had to concentrate so hard on the small things that he didn't pay attention to anything else but the next snap.

"It does feel good to have our fourth win already. We should be able to make the playoffs. Been a long time since we've done that."

"I know. We've already started working on some new cheers just in case we go. "

"I think you better continue practicing them. We can beat both teams."

"It's awesome how much the team has done this year. How's Jason doing?"

"He had a good game. It seemed to click for him. But you know, Jason, he doesn't really talk much. He seems to be doing okay. I don't know though, that would be really hard to go through."

"I know. I can't imagine losing my parents. That would just be horrible."

"Yeah, and Jason and his dad were so close." Troy started to consider what he had just said. How would it feel to actually be that close to your dad? But he shook it off. "Are you ready to go?"

"Yeah, I better get home." Troy stood up first and lifted Ashley's hand as he did. On impulse he decided to kiss her. As she stood up he leaned in and their lips met. For a second nothing mattered. He could taste the lip-gloss she was wearing. He thought it was strawberry. But then she broke the kiss, smiled at him, and said, "I think we better get me home."

Troy couldn't decide if he had done something wrong, or if she was shy, or what. Girls sometimes could make you crazy by the way they reacted to things. Ashley was silent most of the way home. When they pulled up to her house, the porch light was on. She said, "Thanks for a good night." She quickly kissed him on the lips, then darted out of the truck before Troy could do anything. At the door she turned back and motioned for him to call her. He knew already that she meant tomorrow. She didn't take calls after 10:30 at night.

12 GAME EIGHT

The team had a great week of practice. Coach Reiner felt confident that if they played their game they could beat the Bearcats. Last year the Bearcats beat them soundly, but the Vikings had four turnovers in the second half.

This year the Bearcats were sitting three and four. They had had some heartbreaking last-second losses. But Coach Reiner thought their offense was not as powerful as it was last year. They graduated five seniors at skill positions and two on the line.

This was their last away game. The bus ride was quiet, but it was a different type of quiet. It was filled with anticipation. Coach Reiner thought they wanted to be a play-off team. Jason had a good week. There were a couple of moments Coach Reiner noticed during practices that he would drift off, seeing something. Troy seemed to be back to his normal self, a little reckless but striving to get his team to where they needed to be. Coach Reiner found out that he was dating Ashley, a sophomore. He had Ashley in class. He knew she was a solid individual. Smart, quiet, but strong in her beliefs.

He hoped that Ashley's influence could outlast Troy's history. It wasn't easy being a teenager nowadays.

Coach Reiner turned his thoughts back to football. The Bearcats were known for an aggressive defensive style. They were known to be a little bit chippy. They argued every flag. They talked smack, but they could get a team off their game. The Vikings had four personal fouls in last year's game. That next week they had a practice dedicated to understanding smack talk. Coach Reiner wanted them to know the difference between arrogance and confidence. He explained how hitting somebody cleanly and putting them on the ground was more powerful than hitting somebody cheaply. He said the best thing to do is give them a hand-up so their opponent would know they would be back on the next play. The team laughed and joked around, however, the next game he noticed that they were hitting hard and picking the opponents up.

The team was warming up. Coach Reiner walked amongst

them just chatting, asking questions. Jason seemed to be distant when he talked to him. When they moved into their team warm-up section Jason seem to get a little bit agitated with the freshmen, which was normal. Sometimes they would get distracted and chat while the first team was running offensive sets. It was a little uncharacteristic for Jason to snap at them.

Coach Reiner said, "Hey, freshmen, let's make sure you are concentrating on your position." Coach Reiner substituted Rich for Jason and pulled him aside. "You all right?"

"Yes, Coach. I'm fine." But Jason wouldn't look him in the eyes.

"Are you sure, Jason?"

"Yes, Coach. Just getting ready for the game." Jason did look at him then but wouldn't keep eye contact for more than a few seconds

Coach Reiner didn't know if he should push any harder to get Jason to talk. He thought better of it. Right before a game shouldn't be as the time to inquire about how he was doing. Coach patted him on the helmet sending him back in. Coach Reiner mentioned to Coach Sanders to keep an eye on Jason.

The Bearcats won the toss and elected to receive the ball to start the game. The ball was caught at the 5-yard line. The blockers set up a wall on the left hash. Number 27 ran straight for the wall.

The Vikings were not ready for it. The Bearcats returned the opening kickoff for a touchdown. Coach Reiner was uncharacteristically ranting on the sideline. He knew that he had seen two blocks in the back, but there were no flags thrown. Coach Reiner thought to himself that it was going to be a tough one.

The Vikings responded with a 10 play, three minute drive, that ended with a touchdown. Tied game, 7-7.

The game went back and forth. Coach Reiner was agitated; in fact, the whole sideline was in a bad mood. The Bearcats were masters at getting to their opponents. A shove to the head as they got up off the pile. Hits away from the play that, yes, were technically legal but were meant to injure. In pile-ups the Bearcats would twist a foot, give a punch to the groin. The Vikings did all they could not to retaliate.

Coach was trying to keep his team composed; he let them complain longer on the sideline but then reminded them what honor meant and what respect was. That they were playing for something more than getting back at some cheap shot

The Bearcats were up by three at half time, 17 to 14. The team was on edge in the locker room. Even the locker room was irritating. It had once been painted light purple, but now the paint was faded and chipping. In many places you could see the concrete wall. If there was a door left on a locker it was bent in someway that would prevent it from closing.

Jason was quiet. If his mom were here, she would recognize the way his brow was set. As if the sun was just getting into his eyes. Jason was not seeing anyone. His mom would know that he needed space. Teon did not.

"Dog, what's up?"

Jason didn't say anything. Didn't even turn to look at him.

"You all right?" Teon elbowed him. "Man, that number 43 is a jerk, he tried to wrench my knee..."

Jason stood up and walked away.

"Yo? What's up with that?" Teon started to stand up, but Coach Sanders walked over and placed his hand on Teon's shoulder. Coach Sanders looked at him and gave Teon a sad smile. Teon nodded that he understood, but murmured something under his breath.

The second half started with the Vikings getting the ball. Jason was in the zone. Blocking his man, number 63, with every emotion he had. Sometimes driving number 63 four yards down the field. Coach Reiner just followed Jason with fullback dives and counters. In 12 plays the Vikings took the lead 21 to 17.

When the Bearcats took over on offense, Jason continued his dominance. He had a sack on the first play. The Bearcats went three and out.

The Vikings got a good punt return to their own 44. On the first play the Vikings gained 6 yards. Then things turned.

The team lined up on the ball ready for the next play. When the defensive tackle, number 64, set his stance, he looked at Jason in the eyes and said, “How's your dad?”

Without even missing a beat Jason jammed number 64 in the chest, driving him five yards back right into the linebacker. In just seconds both teams were in a fray. Coach Reiner turned quickly to keep the rest of the team on the sideline. He knew this was going to be bad. He stepped onto the field but only a little bit. Yellow flags came raining down. It took five minutes for the referees to separate the two teams. There were small scuffles on each side. The Vikings let the frustration of the first half get the better of them. But the Bearcats weren't backing down either.

Jason was assessed an unsportsmanlike penalty and kicked out of the game. The ramifications of that meant more than just this game. Under the state rules Jason would have to sit out the next game.

For whatever reason, the referees gave offsetting penalties for both teams. But the damage was done, and Jason was gone.

As Coach Reiner led Jason off the field he was deadly silent. Coach Reiner simply looked at him.

Jason said, "He made a comment about my dad."

Coach Reiner didn't have any come back. He knew the Bearcats' reputation for getting under your skin. Coach Reiner didn't know what to say. He trusted what Jason had said. He didn't know exactly how, but he had an urge to pay the Bearcats back. He would think of something. The Vikings ended up punting four plays later.

Coach Reiner called a timeout with one minute left. The Bearcats were about to win the game 24 - 21. The Vikings strived and battled, but without Jason dominating the line, the offense stalled. In fact, it was a good game for the rest of the second half. The Vikings' were now out of time outs. The Bearcats were not trying to score. They were going to simply run out the clock. Coach Reiner gathered the whole team around him. He looked everybody in the eyes before he spoke, "When the end of the game comes, we walk off this field. Do not shake their hands."

The team looked at him. Coach Reiner said, "Sometimes you just have to make a statement. Nobody else will understand but us."

When the final horn went off, the team simply walked to their sideline, gathered their equipment and walked back to the locker room. The Bearcat crowd started to boo. But the Vikings' fans actually broke out into a cheer. They had known something had happened. They knew the character of the Petersen family. They had lost the game, but they had taken another step closer to building their team.

In the locker room Jason was still in his football equipment. He was very quiet. Coach Reiner sat next to him, "You know that you won't be playing in the season finale."

"I know, Coach, but he insulted my father."

"Jason, I wish I could tell you that the world will never try to beat you down, but there will be more situations like this in life. Where you'll simply have to stand against all kinds of negativity."

Jason turned to look at Coach. He couldn't tell if Jason actually heard him or not. He continued, "I know you don't want to hear this but the right road is not the easiest road. And when you lose your head, it may cost you more than a game."

Jason just glared at him. Coach Reiner decided to let it go. It was just too raw of a moment.

Teon texted his mom after the loss. He would be home in about an hour. He was going to go talk with Jason. Teon's mom texted back saying to be careful and that she loved him.

Teon was thinking about how to talk to Jason. He knew that Jason losing his cool on the football field like that was not normal. Something had happened. But he had never had a friend lose such an important person before.

It was difficult to even think about exactly what to say. He knew what it was like not to have a father. He had never known his dad. His dad had left his mom when he was just a baby.

His mother had shown him pictures of his dad. But he felt no connection or relation to the man he saw standing there. Even the one picture where a man was holding a baby Teon in his arms.

Teon wondered what it actually felt like to have somebody you could totally trust. As he thought about it, he fantasized about having a dad. Of coming home and talking about school. Or being able to look on the sideline and see both of his parents standing there. He had a sudden sadness both for Jason and for himself. Jason had lost a father, but at least he knew the beauty of that relationship. Teon had never experienced it.

So as he drove out to the Bend to see if Jason was there, and if he might need a friend.

Jason was sitting on the tailgate of his truck.

“I thought I'd find you here,” Teon said as jumped up on the tailgate.

“Hey.”

“Man, that was a messed up second half. What did that guy say to you?”

“Nothing.”

“I know better than that. You jacked him hard.”

Jason turned to look at Teon. He was really not in the mood.

He didn't want to talk about what was going on in his mind or his heart. The game just didn't seem important. "I don't want talk about it, Teon."

"Come on, dog, what did that dude say?"

Exasperated, Jason gave in, "He asked how my dad was doing."

Teon was silent for a moment, "Sorry, man."

Jason didn't reply; he just stared at the reflection of the moon on the river. He watched as the waves slowly broke the reflection then brought it back together.

"How *are* you?" Teon asked.

He knew that his friend was having a rough time. Two weeks ago he didn't know quite what to do. He knew less now. Teon was surprised at how fast his daily life went back to normal. But he knew that for Jason it was not back to normal yet.

Jason was starting to get irritated. He just wanted to be left alone. Everybody asked how he was doing, or they didn't ask, which actually made him even more frustrated. They know that his dad had died. Everyday he became a little bit angrier as everybody's lives went back to normal. How everybody could laugh. How everybody just went on. Yet, he didn't know exactly what to do next. The house seemed empty. Memories seemed to echo out of every corner. His mom seemed to be doing okay. Friends came and left casseroles or desserts. Sometimes they stayed for coffee. She would go to town everyday. That made Jason mad. How could her life start to be normal? He just wanted to be left alone for a while.

"What did Coach say to you?" Teon kept peppering him with questions.

"Nothing. "

"Hey, you've got to open up a little bit. You can't just hold it all inside. I know things are tough, but we still need you." Teon decided that he would push Jason to talk. He knew that Jason, in fact, his whole family, were quiet, silent types. But it might do some good for him to talk after losing his head during the game.

"I just want to sit here."

"I understand, but you know it's good to get it out into the open."

Jason was getting to a boiling point. He just wanted everything to be back to normal. He wasn't in the mood to listen to Teon. "Leave me alone!"

The situation was getting edgy for Teon; he didn't understand what to say at a time like this. "If you don't want to talk about it, fine, I'm out."

"Why does everybody think that I need to talk it out? You, you don't know how I feel. You wouldn't understand anyway. You never had a father pass away."

Teon froze on the edge of the truck bed as Jason had inadvertently pushed a button. No, Teon had not lost a father because he never had one. "No, because I never had a dad. I do know what it's like to wake up every day without a dad. So maybe it is isn't the same as you, but I know what the hell it feels like."

Jason stared at Teon, shocked by the venom in his voice. Teon decided to continue, "So I know what it's like to try to figure out what's going on. I know what it's like to come home and be proud of something, but nobody's there to share it with. I know what it's like to wonder what you're supposed to do next. To think about what kind of father I'm going to be without anyone to teach me. I know what it's like to live everyday without a dad. You had your dad everyday for seventeen years. So don't tell me that I don't know how it feels. I know how it feels. It hurts, everyday."

Jason looked back at the river, "We're even more alike than I thought."

Teon sat back down, tired from his rant but somehow feeling cleansed to get out what he'd been thinking and feeling for years. "Sorry, you probably didn't deserve all that."

Jason didn't seem to hear him, but he answered, "You know I thought life was this big picture, and everything just went into place. You know like a puzzle. But now that puzzle, my future, everything is just in shambles on the floor. Like somebody has tipped the table and knocked the puzzle over."

Teon was listening. He nodded his head with acknowledgment.

Jason continued, "And right now, I don't even feel like putting the puzzle pieces back in the box. Putting everything back together just seems too hard. I would rather just sit at the table and do nothing."

Teon said, "But we have to... you have to. That's what life is, putting our own puzzles together. Sometimes we have help. But sometimes, I think, we're supposed to do it alone because it is our puzzle. Our picture."

Jason turned to him and said, “But I’m afraid of what the picture will be.”

13 GAME NINE

Coach Reiner called a meeting at the end of practice. "You know that this is our last home game, and this is parents' night." Sam was standing next to him with the clipboards ready to go. "Sam has the clipboards with your name and your parents or guardians' name. You need to check off that the spelling is right. Also you need to indicate how many roses you want. Seniors, you have to mark off if you want a helmet decal for your dad."

For a second Coach Reiner looked toward Jason. He wondered to himself how many times life was going to remind Jason that he lost his father. His senior year, there was parents' night for basketball. Awards night. Graduation. For a moment Coach Reiner's heart went out to Jason. Recognizing that almost every single day he would be reminded that his dad was taken from him.

"We will have the freshman check the spelling first and then sophomores, juniors, and finally seniors. Freshmen, when you're done you need to hit the weight room. Everyone else can head home. Double check the spelling, please."

Coach Reiner watched as they checked off their names. When the seniors came up, Jason asked if he could still get a decal for his dad, Coach Reiner said yes, that would be fine.

Coach Reiner told Sam that he could get a helmet decal for his dad. Coach Reiner had instituted the helmet decal option for fathers for seniors only last year. He knew how important football was to fathers, and he always thought it was odd that mothers always got something on senior night. Sam handed him the clipboard. He saw that a few freshmen forgot to indicate how many roses they needed so he headed to the weight room.

The opposing team had headed to the locker room. Coach Reiner made sure that parents' night happened early in the pregame. He still wanted his team to have as normal start to the game as possible. The announcer called out for all parents of the football team to meet in the north end zone.

Coach Reiner watched as the players went to meet their parents and sometimes younger siblings; the freshmen were wide-eyed but trying to be cool standing next to their parents.

The juniors and seniors were more comfortable showing their affection to their parents. Moms wanted a hug as soon as their son joined them. Events like this showed how a simple game brought families and communities together. Yes, at times it could divide people but only because everyone had a stake in the team.

Teon's mom was making him feel uncomfortable, snapping pictures and making a small scene about how proud she was of him.

Mike was standing alone. He knew that his mom would have to use her dinner break to attend. He hoped that she wasn't called into some type of emergency. He kept his eyes on the entry gate hoping she would get there in time.

Troy stood silently; both of his parents were actually there. Standing on each side of him saying a few words now and then.

Jason and his mom stood silently. You could see that she wanted to be happy for Jason at this moment. But there was an air of sadness around them. A few parents came to say a few words and then headed back to their own little huddle.

Mike was holding the rose for his mom. He was getting even more anxious for her. The announcer started the ceremony with the freshmen. “Number 17, Brad Anderson, the son of Roy and Heather Anderson.”

Mike's mom came dashing through the entry gate. The ticket person didn't even stop her for her entry money. Mike beamed. “I'm not late, am I? It looks like they just started.” They hugged.

Mike said, “You're right on time.” He wondered for a split second what his dad might be doing at this time.

Coach Reiner stood next to his wife. He looked out on his team. Most of the players had both parents. He noticed that there were too many boys without a dad. He counted to himself at least five players in the senior class that were without fathers. And then he looked at Jason. What a challenge some of these boys had just to get through life, let alone to play a football game.

When they got finally to the seniors, the crowd stood up as the announcer broadcast that this was the seniors’ last game.

“And number 56, Jason Petersen, accompanied by his mom. If we could take a moment of silence for Mr. Petersen who we know would have loved to be here tonight.”

The address by the announcer was a surprise to Coach Reiner. Everybody took a moment of silence. Jason and his mom stood at midfield with the whole stadium quiet.

After a few seconds the announcer said, "Thank you. There will be 15 minutes until game time." The speakers switched to music.

The parents hugged their sons tight before they headed back to the stands. The moment of silence for Mr. Petersen reinforced for everybody that this was just a game, but it was a game that brought people together.

Coach Reiner got his team together. "Let's get back to warming up. Offensive groups for five minutes. It's time to put football and our goals on our minds."

The team broke huddle preparing for a chance to end the regular season above .500 and make the playoffs.

"Are you guys ready? This is it. We win this game, and we are in the playoffs. We are above .500. We achieve two more goals. You all know that Jason cannot play this game. But he will be able to play in the first round of the playoffs. So by winning this game you bring Jason back on the field." The team nodded their understanding.

Coach Reiner continued, “This team can be beaten. We're going to attack their outside edge. Landry, number 72, is an all-conference defensive lineman. But our game plan is to chip the outside screens and out passes. But we will have to run to the middle. Kyle, be ready for some battles.” Kyle just nodded yes.

The team was ready. The night air was a bit crisp. You could see the breath of the teams rising above their helmets. You could smell winter in the air. It was a great night for football. It was their last home game of the season. If they did make the playoffs, they would have to travel since they would be a wildcard team.

“Seniors, this is it, no matter what happens, win or lose, this is your last home game. Leave everything on the field.”

Jason stepped up to talk, “I believe in you guys. Let's finish this season right. Team on three. One. Two. Three!”

“Team!” The team broke apart. The kick-off team set up to start the game.

Both teams had come to play. The Mustangs had nothing to lose. They had three wins on this season. Most of their losses were by a touchdown or less. They were a good team. On the first offensive play they completed a 25-yard post route. Then they countered with a sweep that gained 12 yards. Just when it looked like the Mustangs would strike first, Teon intercepted a crossing route, but the ball was jarred loose as he tried to return it. The Mustangs gained possession back. They scored in three plays to take an early lead.

The Vikings scored on their first possession, too. But at a cost. The Vikings were at the Mustangs' 46 yard-line. Coach Reiner called for a screen pass to the left. Mike set the offense. At the snap of the ball, he did a quick five-step drop. The line sold their blocks well and let the defensive linemen go after a count. Landry bit the hardest, thinking he beat Greg, Jason's replacement, with a swim move. The play was unfolding perfectly. Mike backpedaled; his instincts told him to throw the ball, but he held on for one more count, wanting the defensive line as deep as possible. Mike released the ball just before Landry wrapped him up.

The pass was right on target. The offensive linemen didn't have to block anyone until five yards down field. Troy ran untouched to the end zone, and tied the game 7 to 7. But Mike was still laying on the field. As Landry took him to the ground, Mike tried to watch the play so when his body hit the ground his head snapped back hard against the turf.

Coach Reiner jogged out onto the field to check on him, "Mike, you all right?"

"Yeah, Coach. Just enjoying the view," Mike said. He seemed okay as he sat up.

"What day is it, Mike?"

"Friday."

"Who are we playing?" Coach Reiner was asking questions to determine if Mike sustained a concussion when his head hit the ground.

Mike paused before answering, "The Mustangs."

Coach Reiner didn't like the pause, but he gave the right answer. "Repeat this number backwards to me, 5-8-2."

Mike paused again but answered, "2-8-5."

Coach Reiner sighed, "OK, let's get to the sideline." Coach Sanders was there to help Mike up. Coach Reiner told Coach Sanders, "Ethan needs to hold for the extra point."

Coach Reiner told him to go sit on the bench for a minute and get some water. "Sam, go get the EMTs from the ambulance, please."

"Yeah, okay." Sam placed the water bottles on the bench

then jogged to the ambulance in the corner of the north end zone. The EMTs gave Mike a full concussion test on the sideline while the game continued. Ethan, the backup quarterback, was too nervous to make anything happen on offense for the Vikings. The defense held strong but with two minutes left in the second quarter, the Mustangs pulled ahead 14 to 7 with a beautiful 9 route down their own sideline.

The EMTs informed Coach Reiner that Mike passed all the questions and seemed okay. It would be Coach Reiner's call. He gave himself some time by telling Mike they would wait until halftime to make a decision.

Coach Sanders handled the offensive halftime adjustments. Coach Reiner watched Mike's behavior. As Coach Keller discussed the defensive keys, Coach Reiner decided to let Mike play in the second half. The team needed every player they had to win this game. With Jason out they needed to put it all on the line. Coach Reiner reassured himself with what the EMTs said about him passing the concussion test.

The Vikings would start the second half with the ball on the 20 yard line after the Mustangs' outstanding kicker put the ball out of the back of the end zone. Mike was warming up on the sideline.

Coach Reiner motioned for him. "Ace 32 counter."

"Got it, Coach." Mike said as he headed out to the huddle.

The teams lined up. Mike went through his cadence. Things looked good to Coach Reiner. At the snap of the ball Mike turned the wrong way for the play. Since it was a counter, Mike had time to adjust to get the ball into Troy's gut. Six yard gain.

Coach Reiner sent in the next play, Ace 3-4-5-9.

The team broke the huddle with energy. Mike seemed to be going through his pre-snap routine with no problems. His voice sounded confident as he went through the cadence.

"Set, hut!" Mike said. He dropped back and hit Teon on a 5 route, an 8-yard hitch. The problem was that Teon was supposed to run the 3 route, a five-yard out.

Coach Reiner called Mike over to get the play. "Indy 41 Trap, Zip."

"Ok, got it." Mike said turning toward the field.

"Repeat it back to me." Coach Reiner said.

"Huh?"

"Repeat the play to me."

Mike looked confused. He looked at the team huddle and

back to Coach Reiner, "Indy 32 Trap, Zip."

"No, 41 Trap."

"41 Trap, got it."

Coach Reiner grabbed Mike's arm, "Repeat the whole play."

"Ace 41 Zip, Trap."

Quickly, Coach Reiner called a timeout. "Mike, you're not going in."

Mike stared at him. "Coach, I got it. Indy 44 dive. I mean Trap."

Coach Reiner called over the backup quarterback, Ethan. "Indy 41 trap, Zip. Coach Sanders, you got play calling." Mike argued some more as Coach Reiner led him to the bench. Tears were forming in Mike's eyes as he tried to plead his case. Coach Reiner's heart and pride were battling. Winning this game would change everything, but his instincts told him that Mike wasn't okay. Mike might get through the game okay, or another hit could cause serious damage. "Settle down. Sam, we need some water, please." Sam was right there with a water bottle. Jason had joined him.

"Keep an eye on him for me, guys," Coach Reiner said.

"OK, Coach." Sam said as he handed Mike the water bottle.

Jason sat down next to Mike.

Sometimes when a team is against the ropes they shine. The third quarter was an offensive explosion. Behind inspiring play from Ethan, who seemed to have calmed his nerves at half time, the Vikings scored the game-tying touchdown on a beautiful 35-yard post route. The Vikings also scored a field goal on their next series. But the Mustangs came back to take eight minutes off the clock with a 12-play drive that ended with a touchdown and the lead.

To begin the fourth quarter, the Vikings put together another scoring drive. Ethan scrambled on a broken play for 22 yards and the touchdown. The Vikings' defense was fooled by a halfback pass play by the Mustangs late in the fourth quarter. The Vikings found themselves down by four points with four minutes left in the game.

"All right, let's start this drive." Coach Reiner said to the offensive team as they headed out after the kickoff. The Vikings started on their own 26-yard line. Coach Reiner gave Ethan the first play. Houston 30 screen.

Mike was standing next to Coach, "Ethan, you have to bring the D-line to you." Ethan nodded his head in agreement.

Ethan brought the team to the line. "Green 4 … Green 4…."

Ethan looked at the defense, trying to consider the linebacker's position. Ethan trusted his instincts more than any thoughts he had. During JV games he could think through situations easier because the game speed was slower than varsity games. Ethan was trying to keep his frustration at bay. He thought he understood a defense set, but on the snap of the ball a cornerback was in a different spot. He tried not to let overthinking get in his way. "Set… Hut, Hut!"

Houston was their shotgun formation, so Ethan set his feet. Counting one and two in his head, letting the defensive line make their way to him before he started to backpedal. The line was moving quickly to him, and Ethan let the ball go sooner than he wanted. But Troy was there and hollered, "Go" for the linemen. Landry would run Troy down from behind, but not before they gained 12 yards. The home crowd was electrifying. Sneaking a peek at the stands, Coach Reiner saw that no one was sitting, and he smiled. He was enjoying the game. Calling a play, trying to guess what the defense might do. Feeling the anticipation of success.

"What do you think of I Left 8-4-7-2, Mike?" Coach Reiner asked.

Mike had found his way to the sideline and had been giving

his input when asked. He seemed okay, now, but Coach Reiner was at ease with his decision to keep him out of the game, win or lose.

"You're going for the touchdown." Mike looked at Coach Reiner with raised eyebrows. Jason turned to hear the answer.

"Yes, we just gained a first down. Perfect time for it." Mike smiled his agreement.

The defense of the Mustangs ran a gamble, too, on first down. Their gamble won. The Mustangs sent a corner blitz on Ethan's left side, his blind side. Because the pass routes were deeper, Ethan had to hold the ball a second longer. He didn't even sense the cornerback. The Vikings were lucky that Ethan fell on the ball; the corner hit him square in the back rattling the ball from his hands. An 8-yard sack. Coach Reiner kicked himself for that; he almost threw his clipboard but caught himself and had to do a three sixty due to the momentum of his arm. Second down and 18.

"What about a fullback trap?" Mike asked. He took a step back when Coach Reiner turned toward him, not sure how Coach would respond. Mike was enjoying this aspect of football. He didn't know Coach Reiner was so animated on the sidelines. Of course Mike only really saw him before or after a play.

"Good call, Mike." Coach Reiner sent it in. They gained 10 yards. Coach Reiner high-fived Mike. Mike smiled. Third and eight.

Jason agreed, "Nice, Mike."

Coach Reiner wanted to go to their bread and butter play even with Jason out. Indy 33 Dive. Every coach has a set of plays they trust. They know their team will execute the play. But Landry, number 72, was having a great game. The offensive line had to double-team him on most plays.

"Indy 37 Sweep. Tell the tackle and end to Tango block."

Ethan didn't reverse pivot after he pitched the ball to Troy; he wanted to see the play. Randy had a solid block on the corner; Greg and Cam had 72 pinned. Brock turned the corner and got the outside backer. But because the line double-teamed on the defensive line, the middle backer was free. Troy was moving left of the block Daniel made. Five yards, and closing in on the sideline. Troy turned his shoulders to continue up field. Seven yards. That's when Troy collided with number 55, Bruce, the middle linebacker. To the naked eye it looked like two opposite colored waves colliding. Bruce had Troy in a bear hug. Troy leaned into him, pumping his legs as hard as possible. The two of them fell sideways out of bounds right at the yard marker. The stadium went quiet as the referees placed the ball at the hash marker. The chain gang brought out the yard marker and pulled the line straight. The Vikings were two inches short. Decision time.

Coach Reiner called Indy 33 dive 18 bootleg. Ethan was a solid runner. Coach Reiner wasn't worried about that. He was worried about giving the ball to him with so much on the line. It was a gamble, but Coach Reiner knew it was a good call. The Mustangs would be betting on a dive or quarterback sneak. And if you were going to play this game, you'd better be ready.

Mike mumbled, "I can't watch," and went to stand behind Coach Keller.

Ethan turned and gave a great hand fake to Troy as he passed by. For a second Coach Reiner believed he had handed it off. Ethan paused for the slightest second turning his head back toward the play. There was a huge collision at the three hole; Ethan took off to the right at full speed. Keeping the ball into his stomach, he headed for the sideline and the first down. The corner broke off of Teon's block to push Ethan out of bounds, but not before a four-yard gain. First down.

Mike slapped Coach Keller on the shoulders as he jumped up. "Sorry," he said as Coach Keller stared him down for a second, but couldn't hold off a smile.

The clock was down to two minutes 58 seconds. Coach Reiner decided on a passing play on first down. Teon made an outstanding stretched-out catch in the middle of the field for a gain of 18 yards. The home crowd was going crazy. Most of the time Coach Reiner did not hear the crowd, but tonight he relished in their excitement. The whole situation was enhanced. He was aware of everything. He could smell the concession stands and the last few hamburgers from the FFA barbecue in the air. He could hear the student section and the cheerleaders break out into cheers. Coach Reiner may have never felt happier then in moments like this, coaching high school football.

The Vikings were on the Mustangs 32-yard line with plenty of time to finish this drive and take another step in the right program. Coach Reiner reminded himself he didn't need to go for the win just yet. In fact he needed to take off as much time as possible. As if the Mustangs' coach knew what he was thinking, they called a timeout.

Guessing that the Mustangs would believe that they would

run, Coach Reiner decided to pass again. "Indy dive 7-2-8 B flat."

Ethan's main option was actually the fullback going out into the flats.

"Red. 22. Red. 22. Set. Hut!" The Mustangs had called a great blitz on the play. Ethan was too eager to throw the pass and gave a quick ball fake. The middle linebacker was on a read blitz and saw the fake right away.

Ethan felt the pressure coming. He had time to set his feet but threw the ball before he was correctly planted, and it went sailing over Brock's hands. The Mustangs' corner, number 12, saw the play unfold. He made a play on the pass. The ball hit his hands, but as he tried to bring the ball into his chest and run at the same time, he fumbled the ball out of his hands. Disaster avoided.

You could hear a collective sigh come from the home crowd. Second and 10, two minutes 38 seconds.

Coach Reiner called for a halfback sweep. Troy darted toward the sideline after a few yards trying to turn the corner. He toed the line for a few more yards before stepping out of bounds. It was now third and three with two minutes and 18 seconds left.

Coach Reiner called a trap play. Brock easily gained six yards to continue the drive. First and ten on the Mustangs' 28. Two minutes, three seconds. The Mustangs called their second time out. The coach was trying to keep them from running down the clock.

The Mustangs went with an all out blitz stopping Troy for no gain. Coach Reiner noticed that they were stacking six in the box. Going one-on-one coverage on the outside receivers, with two safeties. Without Jason to anchor the left side of the line, he knew that they would either have to go outside or risk another pass play if they were going to get this game.

On second down the Vikings gained three yards on a sweep. Coach Reiner gambled. He thought the Mustangs would probably set their defense for a pass since it was third and long. Coach Reiner sent in the quarterback bootleg. Ethan made a fantastic step jab to make the outside linebacker miss on the 20-yard line. Ethan stepped out of bounds on the 17-yard line. First down. *The crowd could be heard across the state*, Coach Reiner thought.

The energy in the stadium was electrifying. Even the freshmen, who had not seen a second of action, were smiling and high-fiving. Coach Sanders was shouting out encouragement to the players on the field. Coach Keller and Sam were engaged in some type of conversation. Coach Reiner enjoyed the scene for a minute, but then got back to his clipboard. It had been a long time since the team had had a winning season, and Coach Reiner was not going to blow this chance by celebrating too early. If they could get this touchdown and not leave too much time left on the clock, they would have a winning season and a spot in the playoffs.

Coach Reiner decided to run a play action with a rollout with routes that dragged with the quarterback. "Indy 31, Roll 7-4-8."

Ethan set the offensive line. He scanned the defense. Number 48 showed blitz in the left B gap. Ethan thought to himself that that would be just fine. He was feeling confident. The flow of the game had settled his mind. Everything had slowed down for him. The ball fake froze the linebackers. Randy and Teon ran great routes, but with a blitz call on, the defensive backs kept a good cushion on routes.

Ethan had no problem rolling to the outside. The outside linebacker read the roll out and broke to pursue him. Ethan saw that the corner and safety were in the end zone. There was a chunk of open field in front of him. He chose to run.

Teon recognized that Ethan had made the decision to run.

He broke off his route and jammed his hands into the numbers of the corner, driving him to the sideline. The linebacker was pursuing from the left, but Ethan had the speed to rush past him. He headed down the right hash marks. The crowd erupted.

Football is said to be a game of inches. And sometimes those inches define the whole season. It was a foot race with the free safety. Ethan knew that he could get out of bounds at the five-yard line. Or he could go for the win by breaking for the pylon knowing that he would take on a collision with the free safety. Ethan decided to win the game.

The stadium fell silent. All eyes focused on number 8, Ethan, and number 11, Reynolds. Somebody was going to be a hero.

Ethan kept on the hash mark even though he saw number 11 coming from his left. He wanted as much space as possible to make a move when the defender went for the tackle.

Reynolds, a senior, took a pursuit angle at to meet Ethan at about the four-yard line. He had made open field tackles like this before. 'Make sure you get your head on his numbers,' he thought to himself, 'be ready for him to make a cut.'

Seven-yard line. Ethan tightened his grip on the ball. Six-yard line. Reynold slowed his stride while dropping his center of gravity, his hands set for the tackle. Five-yard line.

Ethan tried to wait as long as possible before he made his cut to the right, but Reynold's game experience won out at impact. Ethan felt the hit in his ribs; Reynold smacked him right in the side. Their combined momentum sent them hard right. Ethan kept his legs moving. Reynold tried to lift Ethan up so he could drive him to the ground, but he was too low to get his legs underneath of himself so he kept driving him to the sideline.

Four-yard line. Both crowds started cheering for their team. Willing players on with their voice and heart. Three-yard line. Ethan pushed hard with his legs while working his right arm out with the ball trying to break the plane of the end zone.

Two-yard line. Reynold looked up to see Ethan reach out the ball with his right hand. On instinct, Reynold popped his left hand out and up knocking the ball out of Ethan's hands. With the motion of his arm Reynold's center of gravity changed, causing him to fall. Reynold wrapped Ethan's legs in his right arm, causing Ethan to fall forward. The ball bounced into the end zone just a couple of yards from Ethan's hands. Everything slowed down. Ethan and Reynolds jumped up from the ground scrambling to the ball. Both boys tried to gain an advantage by pushing each other as they scrambled toward the end zone. But the Mustangs' outside linebacker had not given up on the play and sprinted past both of them to fall on the ball. Touchback. The Mustangs would have the ball with a minute left and a four-point lead.

The home crowd let out a sigh. There was a sadness that seemed to envelope the Viking's sideline. Ethan came off the field cursing. Coach Reiner knew he had to get him calmed down. They still had two timeouts left. There was a slim chance.

"Should've just gone out of bounds." Ethan said as he violently snapped off his chinstrap, then yanked his helmet off his head. "What the heck was I doing?"

"Hey, Ethan, there's nothing wrong with going for the win." Coach Reiner knew he had to keep the moment from overtaking Ethan's emotions.

A first down would win the game for the Mustangs. Coach Keller reminded the defense of this. They were going to simply go all out. Nine guys in the box. Get the ball he told them. But the shock of the last play had distracted the team. Jason and Mike tried to lift their spirits, but Coach Reiner could hear the emotion rising in their voices. The Mustangs gained 12 yards on the first play. Coach Reiner called a time out, knowing it didn't really matter. The Mustangs kneeled down on the next play. Coach Reiner called the last timeout.

The locker room was quiet. Many of the players were still in their uniforms, helmets hanging from their hands. Coach Reiner couldn't seem to think. Good things were supposed to happen to good teams. This was a good team. But here they were at the end of the season with four wins, five losses. That close to being above .500. A winning season. A spot in the play-offs.

They had come so far in two years. Funny how success actually highlights failure. Eight wins in two years, more wins then the team had seen in five seasons. But this year was supposed to be a playoff year.

"Coach," Jason said.

"Yes, Jason?" Coach Reiner was surprised.

"I thought this was going to be different. This was supposed to be our year."

Coach Reiner quickly thought of something to say, something

to heal their disappointment. Something inspirational to raise their morale. How do you explain to 17-year-olds that life will never be fair, that you don't always get the breaks? That being great, sometimes, doesn't show up in a win-loss column.

Coach Keller stepped in front of Coach Reiner, “Son, in all my years of coaching, I've never seen a team handle so many hurdles, so many hardships, and still be standing as a team.”

Jason's head lifted. The whole team turned their heads to Coach Keller. Jason responded, “But we didn't make the play-offs.”

“Son,” Coach Keller put his hand on Jason's shoulder. “You're right, we didn't. But look around you. A team, battered and bruised, I'll give you that. But still a team. I'll take this moment, this pain, with you. With all of you.” Coach Keller stepped into the middle of the floor.

“Building a team hurts. Building pride hurts. Losing hurts because of those two things. I remember just a few years ago when this room would have been filled with laughter and music after a loss. It didn't hurt because there was no team. There was no pride.”

The upperclassmen murmured their agreement. They remembered how disconnected and easy losing used to be.

"I know this hurts, but you need this pain. Not just now, but someday as a father, a husband, even as a friend. This pain is growth, men. It means you are working hard for something. Coach Reiner will hate this, but Coach Sanders won't. Football is over, but team is not. Many of you will be starting basketball, and I hope you take this moment with you into that season... that you take this team with you."

The players were stuck between inspiration and the pain of the loss. They started to talk amongst themselves. Coach Reiner moved to speak to the team, but then thought better of it. Sometimes coaches can talk too much.

The three coaches walked to the office.

The locker room never got loud, but laughter and stories of the game found their way back into the room. Coach Reiner was sitting at his desk. He was still trying to accept the ending of the season. He knew that the team had done some great things. Yes, the record was the same as last year, but they were two yards away from going to the playoffs.

Coach Reiner headed out to the locker room. It was silent.

Scraps of tape and pre-wrap littered the floor along with bottles of Gatorade and wrappers from Power Bars. Jess, the freshman QB, didn't lock his locker, again. Coach Reiner sighed; Jess was going to be a project. He was already six foot, had a great arm, but was scattered brained. Coach Reiner snapped the lock. Already thinking about next season. He turned back to the office and jumped.

The seniors were standing there. Jason stepped forward reaching his hand out to shake Coach Reiner's.

"Thank you, Coach."

Each player stepped forward repeating the simple acknowledgement, "Thank you, Coach."

Coach Reiner couldn't speak; he didn't need to.

They were sitting on a park bench. This was becoming one of their favorite places to go. The night was a little bit chilly and they could see their breath in the air.

"You guys should be proud. You had a good year. I've never seen the team play so well." Ashley said.

"But we ended up with the exact same record as last year. It didn't matter how well we played." Troy bent down with his head in his hands.

"I know you didn't do everything you thought you were going to. But you have to know that you played well."

Troy's emotions were bubbling up. It wasn't that he wasn't proud, but he and the team believed they would have a better season. They expected better of themselves. That was the thing that most bothered Troy, that he didn't rise to the occasion. The team didn't achieve what they could have. Then Troy heard his dad's voice in his head telling him that he told him so, that he would never be as good as him.

That voice drove Troy over the edge. He was mad. Ashley tried to stand up and hold his hand, but Troy defiantly shook her off and stormed away, leaving Ashley to find her own way home. Troy was trying to run from his dad's voice. But the record of the team proved his dad was right.

To make matters more confusing, through the haze of his dad's voice he could remember the lessons of the season. He could hear Coach Reiner's message. Nothing was ever guaranteed. That hard work was the only control that you truly had, and that success was sometimes measured away from the scoreboard

Coach Reiner's voice was easily flooded out with the rage of his dad's voice, with the knowledge of the team record, and the flashes of everyday life with his mom and dad.

Troy desperately did not want to be like his dad. When he looked in the rearview mirror, all he saw was his father's reflection.

EPILOGUE

The snow was falling gently, big fluffy flakes. David was watching the flakes from the kitchen window. He was cleaning the lunch dishes and keeping an eye on the apple cider. He was feeling antsy. It had been two weeks since the end of the season and he wasn't used to the freedom of a Sunday afternoon. No game tapes to watch, no game planning with the other coaches. He did have some schoolwork to grade, but that could wait.

His wife was in high spirits. "Is the cider ready?"

David dried his hands. The sweet tang of cider filled the room. "Yes, I think it is."

Julie grabbed two mugs from the cupboard. David poured the apple cider from the pan. Lifting it up and back down like a bar tender would a bottle. He spilled down the side of his wife's cup.

“The first snow of the year.” His wife said as she grabbed some paper towels to clean up the cider.

“Yea, we've had a good fall, weather wise.” David was feeling good. The football season was still on his mind. Like any coach he was thinking about next season, but for today he would be a husband and not a coach.

“What time is the Minnesota game?” Julie asked.

“They play Monday night. No football this afternoon.”

His wife smiled, and patted the seat cushion next to her on the couch. “Music?” she asked.

David turned on the stereo. “So, what should we talk about?” he asked as he sat next to his wife.

“Nothing,” she said as she leaned into him. He lifted his left arm to wrap around her and let the silence take over for a while.

Twenty minutes later they were reminiscing. Laughing at some memory of a tough time that with the passing of time became a funny story when there was a knock at the door. David got up, shrugging toward his wife. It was still snowing; the flakes slowly but steadily piling up on the ground.

He opened the door to find most of the football team

scrunched together on his porch with a football in Jason's hands. "Hey, Coach. Most of the team is headed to the practice field. We thought maybe you would like to play some football with us. It's great weather for it." A genuine smile broke across Jason's face.

David turned to look at his wife. She stood there with a freshly poured cup of apple cider, frowning at him. His heart sank. He knew that the football season was a challenge for her, too. But she couldn't hold the frown long, a smile cracked across her face. She said, "Yes, you can go play."

Coach Reiner felt like a sixth grader getting the chance to go out unexpectedly to play. "Let me grab my coat." Then he stopped, and he asked, "What about Coach Sanders and basketball?"

Coach Sanders stepped into view with Coach Keller just off his shoulder, "Coach, sometimes it's all right to play."

Coach Reiner grabbed his fleece and his gloves from the closet, hurriedly got his boots, and headed out into the snow to play.

"But, we are not tackling, one hand touch," Coach Sanders hollered as they left the porch.

Julie watched him leave. Placing her hand on her stomach, she thought to herself that the news could wait.

ABOUT THE AUTHOR

Jamey Boelhower is a husband and father of six. He has been coaching for 20 years. Jamey started his coaching career with the Hastings College track team. When Jamey started teaching high school English, he coached football, basketball, and track. Jamey has been writing since the fourth grade. He has a blog, It is All Connected, where he shares his insights on life. This is his first novel.

Made in the USA
Lexington, KY
12 April 2015